Also by Rachael Reed

Sis
Sis 2 Blood on the Streets

Standalone
Codefendant
Codefendant
Once a Cheater
Once a Cheater
Passport Bro
What Happens in Prison
Preference
Sprinkle Sprinkle
Championship Bad
Street Exodus
Street Exodus
Street Royalty
Pawns of Power
SIS
Cartel Bloodline
Get Money Girls
Skip the Games
Til Death Do Us Part

Backpage Hustle
Link in Bio
The Virgin and The Kingpin
A Gangsta's Heart
Boosters
Can't Turn a Hoe Into a Housewife
Better you Than Me
Wig Dealer: How to Start Your wig Business
Trail Ride Blues

Trail Ride Blues

Trail Ride Blues

By Rachael Reed

Copyright © 2024 by Rachael Reed

Check Out More Great Products and Free Giveaways
https://tbdbpublishing.com/

Chapter 1: The Perfect Life

Priscilla sat on the wraparound porch of her ranch, the soft breeze playing with the hem of her sundress. The sun was setting behind the rolling hills, casting a golden glow across the fields where her husband, Marcus, was working with the horses. She sipped her sweet tea, feeling every bit the Southern belle she was raised to be. Life was perfect.

Priscilla had it all. A husband who was a legend in the rodeo world, a beautiful home, and a thriving social media presence that made her the envy of women all over the country. Her Instagram was a constant stream of perfectly curated moments—her in front of the barn with a pitchfork, her in the kitchen baking pies, her on horseback, her long hair flowing behind her like some kind of fairy tale princess. To her hundreds of thousands of followers, she was the epitome of grace and elegance, the very definition of Southern charm.

But all that glittered wasn't gold.

The truth was, Priscilla had been living in a bubble, one carefully constructed by Marcus and herself. They were the perfect couple, or so it seemed. Behind closed doors, though, the pressure of maintaining that image was starting to weigh heavy on her. The ranch life, the social media, the constant need to be "on" all the time—it was exhausting. And while Marcus was the man of every woman's dreams on the outside, behind that cowboy hat was a man as cold as the steel spurs on his boots.

But she kept on, smiling for the cameras, posting for the likes. Because that's what she was supposed to do. That's what she was trained to do. In the South, you didn't let the world see you sweat. You didn't let them see your tears. And Lord knows, you didn't let them see your secrets.

Priscilla's phone buzzed on the table next to her, breaking her out of her thoughts. She picked it up, her heart skipping a beat when she saw Marcus' name on the screen.

"Hey baby," she said, her voice sweet as honey, masking the nervous flutter in her stomach.

"Where you at?" Marcus' voice was rough, his Southern drawl more pronounced than usual.

"On the porch, why? Somethin' wrong?"

"Come inside. We need to talk."

Her heart dropped into her stomach. Marcus wasn't one for heart-to-hearts. If he said they needed to talk, it wasn't good. Priscilla stood up, smoothing her dress down as she walked into the house. She found him in the living room, standing by the fireplace, a manila envelope in his hand. His face was set in a hard line, his eyes cold as ice.

"What's goin' on?" she asked, trying to keep her voice steady.

Marcus didn't answer right away. He just stared at her, his jaw clenched. Finally, he tossed the envelope onto the coffee table in front of her. "Open it," he said, his voice low.

Priscilla's hands shook as she reached for the envelope. She slid her fingers under the flap and pulled out a DVD. No label, nothing to indicate what it was. She looked up at Marcus, confused. "What is this?"

"Put it in the player," he said, his eyes never leaving her.

She hesitated, something inside her screaming not to do it. But she knew better than to argue with Marcus when he was like this. She walked over to the DVD player and slid the disc in, her heart pounding in her chest. The TV screen flickered to life, and for a moment, all she saw was static. Then the video began to play.

Priscilla's breath caught in her throat as she watched herself on the screen, naked and writhing in the middle of an orgy. The men surrounding her were faceless, shadows in the dimly lit room, but there was no mistaking who the woman was. The long braids, the body type, the voice—it was all her. Or at least, it looked like her.

Her knees buckled, and she had to grab onto the edge of the table to keep from collapsing. "That... that ain't me," she whispered, her voice shaking.

Marcus snorted, his lips curling into a sneer. "Really? 'Cause it damn sure looks like you. And it sounds like you, too."

Tears welled up in her eyes, but she blinked them back, refusing to let them fall. "I swear, Marcus, I don't know what this is. I ain't never... I would never..."

"Bullshit!" he snapped, his voice like a whip. "You been playin' me for a fool, ain't you? All them trail rides, all them nights you said you was just hanging out dancing—this is what you was doin', huh?"

"No! I swear to God, I ain't never done nothin' like this in my life!" She was crying now, the tears spilling down her cheeks as she pleaded with him. "You gotta believe me, Marcus, please..."

But Marcus was done listening. He turned away from her, his shoulders tense, his hands balled into fists. "I don't know who you are anymore, Priscilla," he said, his voice cold. "But I sure as hell know who you ain't. You ain't the woman I married. You ain't the woman I thought you was."

Priscilla sank to the floor, her body trembling as the weight of his words crushed her. She couldn't breathe, couldn't think. All she could do was watch as her perfect life shattered into a million pieces around her.

The sound of the front door slamming shut echoed through the house, and Priscilla knew that Marcus was gone. For the first time in her life, she felt truly alone. And as she sat there on the floor, surrounded by the remnants of her broken world, one thought kept running through her mind:

That ain't me in that video, then who the hell is it?

The question burned in her mind, twisting her insides into knots. She had no memory of ever being in that room, no recollection of those men, those touches or even of that night. But the woman on the screen—she was a spitting image of her, down to the last detail.

Could it be someone trying to ruin her? Someone who looked just like her? The thought was insane, impossible, but so was everything else that was happening.

Priscilla's mind raced as she tried to piece together what little she knew. The walls of her perfect life were closing in on her, suffocating her with each passing second. She needed answers. She needed to find out who was behind this, before it destroyed everything she had.

She stumbled to her feet, her legs weak beneath her. She needed to think, to clear her head. But the only thought that kept coming back was the look in Marcus' eyes as he walked out the door. The look of a man who had been betrayed in the worst possible way.

With a deep breath, Priscilla wiped the tears from her face and squared her shoulders. She was going to find out the truth, no matter what it took. And when she did, she was going to make sure that whoever was responsible paid for what they'd done.

Because if there was one thing Priscilla knew, it was that you didn't mess with her and get away with it.

This was just the beginning.

Chapter 2: Shattered Image

Priscilla could barely sleep that night. The images from the video kept replaying in her mind, the shock of seeing herself—or someone who looked exactly like her—in that filthy scene. The shame and confusion gnawed at her, twisting her insides into knots. Marcus hadn't come back to the house. She'd called him, texted him, but there was nothing but silence. She couldn't blame him, really. If she were in his shoes, she might've reacted the same way. But the fear that she might never be able to clear her name, that she might lose everything because of something she didn't do, was suffocating.

When morning came, Priscilla felt like a shell of herself. She dragged herself out of bed, her eyes bloodshot from crying all night. She moved like a ghost through the house, each step heavy with dread. The life they'd built together felt like it was crumbling beneath her feet.

Around noon, Marcus finally walked through the door. His boots clattered loudly against the wooden floor, and Priscilla's heart jumped into her throat. She hurried to the living room, her stomach twisting with a mixture of hope and fear. But the moment she saw his face, she knew this wasn't going to be a reconciliation.

Marcus looked like he hadn't slept either. His eyes were red, his jaw clenched tight. He had that wild look in his eyes, like he was ready to tear everything apart. He didn't say a word as he stormed past her, heading straight for the liquor cabinet. He grabbed a bottle of whiskey, yanked the top off, and took a long swig, the liquid burning down his throat.

"Marcus…" Priscilla's voice trembled as she tried to approach him, but he shot her a look so cold it froze her in her tracks.

"Don't," he snarled, his voice low and dangerous. "Don't you even start, Priscilla."

Tears welled up in her eyes, but she blinked them back. "I swear to God, I don't know what that video is. I've never done anythin' like that. You gotta believe me, Marcus. Please."

"Believe you?" He laughed bitterly, the sound harsh and cruel. "You expect me to believe that bullshit? You think I'm stupid, huh? That I don't know what I saw?"

Priscilla shook her head, her hands trembling as she reached out to him. "No, baby, I don't think you're stupid. I just... I don't know what this is, but it ain't me. I would never hurt you like that."

"Then who is it?" he snapped, slamming the bottle down on the table. "Who the fuck is it if it ain't you? 'Cause she looks just like you. Same hair, same voice, same fuckin' tattoo on her back. You tellin' me you that aint you?"

Priscilla's heart skipped a beat at his words. How could someone orchestrate something so elaborate just to destroy her life?

"I don't know," she whispered, her voice barely audible. "But I swear, Marcus, I ain't never been with no one else. I love you. I'd never cheat on you. You gotta believe me."

"Believe you?" Marcus's voice cracked with emotion, and for a moment, Priscilla saw the hurt beneath the anger. "How the hell am I supposed to believe you after seein' that? You expect me to just forget it, to just pretend it didn't happen?"

"No!" Priscilla cried, her voice desperate. "I just... I don't know how to prove it to you, but it's the truth. You know me, Marcus. You know I wouldn't do this."

Marcus turned away from her, his shoulders tense. He ran a hand through his hair, trying to keep himself together. But the doubt, the anger, it was eating him alive. "I don't know what I know anymore," he muttered, his voice thick with emotion. "Everything I thought was real... it's all fucked up now."

Priscilla's heart shattered at his words, the pain cutting through her like a knife. She wanted to hold him, to make him believe her, but the chasm between them felt too wide, too deep.

"Marcus..." she whispered, but he shook his head, cutting her off.

"Don't, Priscilla. Just... don't." He picked up the bottle again, taking another long drink. "I need some time. I need to think."

"Think about what?" she asked, panic rising in her chest. "You can't just walk away from me. We need to figure out who did this to us. We need to—"

"We?" Marcus interrupted; his voice harsh. "There ain't no 'we' right now. This video is every fuckin where Im the laughin fuckin stock and I need to figure out what the fuck I'm gonna do with my life, 'cause right now, I don't know if I can keep doin' this."

The words hit her like a punch to the gut, and Priscilla stumbled back, her eyes wide with shock. "You can't mean that," she whispered, her voice breaking. "You don't mean that, Marcus. We can get through this. We can..."

But Marcus wasn't listening. He was already walking away, leaving her standing there, alone and broken. She watched as he grabbed his keys off the counter and headed for the door, her heart racing with fear.

"Marcus, please," she begged, her voice hoarse. "Don't do this. Don't leave me."

He paused at the door, his back to her. For a moment, she thought he might turn around, that he might give her a chance. But then he spoke, his voice cold and distant. "I ain't leavin' you. I just don't wanna be around you right now."

And with that, he was gone again, the door slamming shut behind him.

Priscilla stood there, frozen in place, the silence of the house pressing down on her like a weight. She felt like she was drowning, the walls closing in on her, the life she'd known slipping through her fingers. How had everything fallen apart so fast? How had they gone from being the perfect couple, the envy of everyone they knew, to this?

She sank down onto the couch, her body trembling as the reality of the situation hit her. Marcus didn't believe her. The man she loved more than anything in the world, the man she'd built her life with, thought she was a liar, a cheater. And no matter how much she pleaded, no matter how many times she told him the truth, he couldn't get past what he'd seen.

This video was making its round and clips of it were going viral online. What about the rest of the world? What would they think about this? Priscilla had worked so hard to build her brand, to cultivate an image of perfection. She was the Southern belle, the ranch wife, the influencer who had it all. But all it took was one video, one lie, to bring it all crashing down.

She could already hear the whispers, the gossip spreading like wildfire through their social circles. People loved nothing more than to tear down those they envied, and Priscilla knew she'd given them the perfect ammunition. The thought of facing them, of seeing the judgment in their eyes, made her stomach churn.

And then there was social media. Her entire career was built on the image she presented online. What would happen when her followers found out? Would they believe her, or would they turn on her too? Would they see her as the perfect wife, the gracious hostess, or would they see her as the woman in that video, a liar, a fraud?

Priscilla's phone buzzed again, and she stared at it with dread. She knew what was coming. The calls, the messages, the questions she couldn't answer. But she couldn't ignore it forever. She reached for the phone with a shaking hand, her heart pounding in her chest as she opened the message.

It was from one of her sponsors. The message was short, cold, to the point. They were "reconsidering their partnership" in light of recent events. Priscilla's stomach dropped, the words blurring in front of her eyes. This was just the beginning. The sponsors, the deals, the money—it was all going to disappear. Everything she'd worked so hard for, everything she'd sacrificed for, was slipping away.

Priscilla threw the phone across the room, the device crashing against the wall with a satisfying smash. But the relief was fleeting. The anger, the frustration, the fear—it all came rushing back, overwhelming her. She buried her face in her hands, the sobs wracking her body.

How had it all gone so wrong? How had she lost everything in the blink of an eye?

But even through the tears, one thought burned in her mind. She had to find out the truth. She had to figure out who was behind this, who had done this to her. Because if she didn't, if she let this lie destroy her, she'd never be able to look at herself in the mirror again.

Priscilla lifted her head, wiping the tears from her face. She wasn't going to let this break her. She wasn't going to let them win. She was going to fight back, no matter what it took. And when she found the person responsible, they were going to pay.

Chapter 3: Ghosts from the Past

Priscilla sat alone in the dimly lit living room, the silence of the house pressing down on her like a weight. The echoes of the past few days reverberated in her mind, each memory sharp and painful. Marcus was gone, her reputation was hanging by a thread, and the life she had built with such care was crumbling beneath her. She felt like she was drowning, each breath harder to take than the last. But amidst the chaos, a single thought kept gnawing at her: the woman in the video. Who was she? How could she look so much like Priscilla?

She reached for her phone, her fingers trembling as she scrolled through her contacts. She needed to talk to someone, someone who might help her make sense of the madness. Her thumb hovered over Keisha's name, her best friend since childhood. Keisha had always been there for her, through thick and thin, the one person who would listen without judgment.

Priscilla hesitated, her finger trembling above the screen. What if Keisha didn't believe her? What if she, too, thought Priscilla was lying? But she couldn't keep this to herself any longer. She needed help, needed someone to tell her she wasn't crazy. She pressed the call button, her heart pounding as the phone rang.

"Girl, what's good?" Keisha's voice crackled through the speaker, her tone light and carefree, oblivious to the storm brewing in Priscilla's life.

"Keisha," Priscilla whispered, her voice shaky. "I... I need to talk to you. It's bad, real bad."

There was a pause on the other end, the weight of Priscilla's words sinking in. "What happened, Cilla? You sound like you just saw a ghost."

Priscilla took a deep breath, trying to steady herself. "I think I did."

"Hold up, what you talkin' 'bout?" Keisha's voice was laced with concern now, the lightness gone.

Priscilla closed her eyes, the image of the video flashing in her mind. "Somebody sent Marcus a video, Keisha. A video of me... or someone who looks just like me, doing... doing things I ain't never done in my life."

Keisha was silent for a moment, processing what Priscilla had said. "Wait, hold up. You mean to tell me somebody out here playin' with your face like that? You sure it ain't you?"

Priscilla's voice trembled as she answered, "I swear to God, Keisha, it ain't me. I don't remember any of it. But the woman... she looks just like me. Same hair, same voice, everything. It don't make no sense."

"Damn, girl," Keisha muttered, the shock evident in her voice. "That's some next-level shit. You think somebody out there tryin' to set you up?"

"I don't know," Priscilla replied, her voice breaking. "But it got me thinkin'... what if there's someone out there who looks just like me? It's like some long lost twin type shit goin on I swear.

Keisha's voice dropped to a whisper, her tone serious. "Twin? Cilla, you been watchin' too much TV."

Priscilla shook her head, even though Keisha couldn't see her. "I don't know, Keisha. I was adopted, remember? My mama never told me nothin' 'bout no twin, but what if... what if there's somethin' she didn't tell me? What if there's more to my past than I know?"

Keisha sighed, the sound heavy with concern. "Girl, you know I love you, but this sound crazy. But... I guess it ain't impossible. You ever look into your real family? You ever try to find out where you come from?"

Priscilla bit her lip, the memories of her childhood flooding back. She had always known she was adopted, but her parents had been good to her, given her everything she could ever want. She had never felt the need to dig into her past, never questioned where she came from. But now, with everything falling apart, she realized how little she really knew about herself.

"No," Priscilla admitted, her voice small. "I never looked. I didn't wanna know. I was happy, you know? I didn't think it mattered."

"Well, it matters now," Keisha said firmly. "If there's a twin out there, you need to find out. You need to know who this bitch is, 'cause she out here tryin' to fuck ya life up. You can't just sit back and let this shit happen."

Priscilla nodded, determination flickering to life inside her. "You right, Keisha. I gotta find out the truth. But I don't even know where to start."

"Start with your folks," Keisha suggested. "Maybe they know somethin'. And if they don't, you can hire somebody to look into it for you. But you gotta do somethin', Cilla. You can't let this go."

Priscilla knew Keisha was right. She couldn't just sit around and wait for her life to fall apart. She had to take control, had to find out who was behind this. She had to find out exactly what was goin on.

"I'll start with my parents," Priscilla said, determination hardening her voice. "I'll talk to them, see if they know anything. And if they don't, I'll hire someone to dig into my past. I ain't gonna let this ruin me, Keisha. I'm gonna fight back."

"That's my girl," Keisha said, her voice full of support. "You ain't alone in this, Cilla. You need anything, you call me. We gon' get through this together."

"Thanks, Keisha," Priscilla whispered, tears of gratitude filling her eyes. "I don't know what I'd do without you."

"Girl, please," Keisha laughed, the sound a welcome relief from the tension. "We been through worse than this. You just stay strong, aight? We gon' get to the bottom of this shit."

Priscilla hung up the phone, a sense of determination settling over her like a heavy cloak. She knew what she had to do now. She couldn't sit back and let her life be destroyed by some faceless enemy. She had to take action, had to dig into the past she had long ignored.

But as she sat there, the weight of the task ahead of her pressing down on her, she couldn't shake the feeling of unease that had settled in her stomach. The idea of someone who looked just like her but was living a completely different life, sent shivers down her spine. What kind of person would do something like this? What kind of life had this person led, to end up so bitter, so vengeful?

Priscilla stood up, her legs feeling like lead as she made her way to the bookshelf in the corner of the room. There, hidden behind rows of carefully curated books, was a small wooden box. She pulled it out, her hands trembling as she opened the lid.

Inside were old papers, letters, and photographs—pieces of a life she had long since left behind. Her adoption papers were there, yellowed with age, the edges worn from years of being handled. She pulled them out, her eyes scanning the faded text. Her birth name was there, the name she had been given before she was adopted: Ramona.

Priscilla's heart skipped a beat as she read the name. It was the first time she had seen it in years, the name she had tried to forget. Ramona. She had always known it was her birth name, but she had never thought much about it. It was just a name, a relic of a past that didn't belong to her anymore.

But now, as she stared at the name, a chill ran down her spine. What if... what if there was another Ramona out there? A twin, someone who had been given the same name but lived a completely different life? The thought sent a wave of fear crashing over her, the implications too terrifying to fully comprehend.

Priscilla shoved the papers back into the box, her hands shaking. She couldn't deal with this right now. She needed answers, needed to know who she really was, and where she came from. But the fear, the uncertainty, it was too much to bear. She felt like she was standing on the edge of a cliff, the ground crumbling beneath her feet.

She needed to talk to her parents, needed to confront them about the past they had always kept hidden from her. But she was afraid of what she might find out. What if they had lied to her? What if everything she thought she knew about herself was a lie?

Priscilla shook her head, trying to push the fear aside. She couldn't let it paralyze her. She had to move forward, had to find out the truth. And no matter what it took, she was going to get to the bottom of this.

She picked up the phone again, her fingers shaking as she dialed her parents' number. The phone rang, the sound echoing in the silence of the house. Her heart pounded in her chest, each ring drawing her closer to the moment of truth.

Finally, her mother's voice came through the line, warm and familiar. "Hello?"

"Mom," Priscilla said, her voice trembling. "I need to talk to you. It's important."

Chapter 4: The Search for Ramona

Priscilla sat in her car, her hands gripping the steering wheel so tight her knuckles turned white. The engine idled, the soft hum the only sound in the otherwise silent night. She had been sitting there for nearly an hour, parked outside the small, nondescript building that housed the office of a private investigator. Her mind was racing, her thoughts tangled in a web of fear, desperation, and a growing sense of dread.

She had never imagined she'd find herself in a place like this, needing to hire someone to dig into her past, to uncover secrets she had long buried. But after her conversation with her parents, the doubts that had gnawed at her since the video surfaced only grew stronger. They had been vague, evasive, clearly hiding something. And that something was eating away at Priscilla, driving her to this moment.

Taking a deep breath, she finally turned off the engine and stepped out of the car, her legs trembling as she walked toward the door. The night air was cool, a stark contrast to the heat bubbling up inside her. She pushed open the door and stepped inside, the scent of stale coffee and cigarette smoke hitting her as she entered the dingy office. A single desk lamp cast a dim glow over the room, highlighting the stacks of papers and old case files that littered every surface.

A man looked up from behind the desk, his eyes narrow and calculating. He was rough around the edges, with a five o'clock shadow that hadn't seen a razor in days and a cigarette dangling from his lips. His name was Detective Alonzo "Big Al" Ramirez, and he was known for getting the job done, no matter what it took.

"You Priscilla Johnson?" he asked, his voice rough, like gravel scraping against concrete.

"Yeah, that's me," she replied, trying to steady her voice.

He nodded toward the chair across from him. "Sit down. Tell me what you need."

Priscilla hesitated for a moment, then took a seat. Her stomach churned as she tried to find the words to explain what she needed, what she was looking for. "I need you to find someone," she finally said, her voice barely above a whisper. "Someone I didn't know existed until now."

Big Al raised an eyebrow, his expression skeptical. "You lookin' for an old boyfriend or somethin'?"

"No," Priscilla shook her head, her throat tight. "I think... I think I might have a twin sister. We were separated at birth. I don't know where she is, or even if she's still alive. But I need to find her. It's... it's important."

Alonzo leaned back in his chair, his eyes narrowing as he studied her. "A twin, huh? You sure about that?"

Priscilla nodded, her heart pounding in her chest. "I don't know for sure, but... I have reason to believe she's out there."

Big Al took a drag from his cigarette, the smoke curling around his head like a halo. "That's heavy shit, girl. You got any leads? Anythin' that might help me find her?"

Priscilla fumbled in her bag, pulling out the adoption papers she had found in the wooden box. She handed them to Big Al, her hands shaking. "This is all I got. My birth name was Ramona. I don't know her exact name, but it's a start."

Big Al took the papers, glancing over them before nodding. "Aight, I'll see what I can do. But this ain't gonna be cheap. You sure you wanna go down this road?"

"I don't have a choice," Priscilla said, her voice firm despite the fear gnawing at her insides. "I need to know the truth about alot."

Big Al nodded, his expression serious. "Aight, then. I'll get to work. I'll be in touch when I find somethin'."

Priscilla stood, her legs shaky beneath her. "Thank you," she said, her voice barely audible. "I appreciate it."

Big Al just nodded, already focused on the papers in front of him. As Priscilla walked out of the office, the weight of what she had just set in motion pressed down on her like a ton of bricks. She had just opened a door she might never be able to close again.

The days dragged on, each one filled with a gnawing sense of dread that only grew stronger with each passing hour. Marcus was distant, barely speaking to her, his eyes cold and accusing every time they crossed paths. Priscilla could feel the walls of their marriage closing in around her, suffocating her with the weight of everything unsaid, unresolved. She tried to reach out to him, tried to explain, but it was like talking to a brick wall. He had already made up his mind, and nothing she said would change that.

Meanwhile, the whispers grew louder, more vicious. The once-friendly smiles of neighbors and acquaintances were now replaced with sneers and judgmental stares. Priscilla couldn't even go to the grocery store without feeling the eyes on her, the low murmurs that followed her wherever she went. Her perfect life was unraveling, and there was nothing she could do to stop it.

Then, one afternoon, her phone rang. It was Big Al. Priscilla's heart leaped into her throat as she answered, her hands trembling. "Did you find something?" she asked, her voice shaking with anticipation.

"Yeah, I found something," Big Al replied, his voice grim. "I think it's your twin. Her name's Rachel. She's been livin' in the projects on the south side. It ain't pretty, Priscilla. This girl's been through hell and back."

Priscilla's breath caught in her throat as she listened, her mind racing. "Tell me everything," she whispered.

Big Al took a deep breath, his voice heavy with the weight of what he was about to reveal. "Rachel's life ain't nothin' like yours. She grew up in the system, bounced around from foster home to foster home. She's been in and out of juvie, then prison. Drugs, gangs, you name it, she's seen it. She's got a rap sheet a mile long."

Priscilla felt like the ground was falling out from under her. "At me? Why? I never even knew she existed."

Big Al continued. "She knows about you. Always has. She's been watchin' you from the sidelines, seein' you live this life she never had."

Priscilla's heart pounded in her chest, the pieces of the puzzle slowly clicking into place. "So, do you think she's the one who made that video? Is she the one tryin' to ruin me?"

Big Al sighed. "It's lookin' that way. She's been usin' your name, your face, all kinda shit. One a few criminal reports she gave your name. This girl ain't playin' around, Priscilla. She seems dangerous. She's got nothin' to lose, and that makes her unpredictable."

Priscilla's mind raced as she tried to process everything Big Al was telling her. The thought of someone out there, someone who looked just like her, someone who hated her enough to destroy her life—it was too much to bear. "What do I do?" she whispered, her voice trembling with fear.

Big Al was silent for a moment before answering. "You need to be careful, Priscilla. This ain't just some jealous sister rivalry. This is serious. Rachel's been livin' in the streets, she knows how to survive, and she won't go down without a fight. You need to watch your back."

Priscilla felt the fear grip her heart, cold and unrelenting. She had to find Rachel had to confront her, but the thought of coming face-to-face with this stranger who shared her face and wanted nothing more than to destroy her for no reason filled her with dread. "I need to see her," she said, her voice barely audible. "I need to talk to her, find out why she's doing this."

Big Al hesitated. "You sure about that? This girl ain't right in the head, Priscilla. She's been through some shit that messed her up real bad. You might not like what you find."

"I don't care," Priscilla replied, her voice firm despite the fear coursing through her veins. "I need to end this. I need to know is she doing this to me."

Big Al sighed again, the sound heavy with resignation. "Aight, I'll set it up. But be careful, Priscilla. You're walkin' into a lion's den."

Priscilla hung up the phone, her mind spinning. She knew what she had to do, but the thought of it filled her with a sense of dread so deep it felt like it might swallow her whole. She was about to confront the ghost from her past, a ghost that had been lurking in the shadows of her life, waiting for the right moment to strike.

As she sat there, the weight of the situation pressing down on her, she knew there

Chapter 5: Revelations and Revenge

Rachel leaned against the cracked wall of her dingy apartment, a cigarette dangling from her lips. The glow from the cheap neon sign outside her window cast a sickly green light across the room, illuminating the peeling wallpaper and the threadbare furniture. The place reeked of stale smoke, sweat, and desperation. It was a far cry from the life she had imagined for herself, but it was all she had ever known.

She took a long drag from the cigarette, her mind racing as she looked onto social media and seen Priscilla. Her twin sister, the one who had everything, handed to her on a silver platter while Rachel had to fight tooth and nail just to survive. It wasn't fair. It had never been fair. And now, after all these years, she was finally going to make things right.

She had been watching Priscilla for years, ever since she had first found out about her. Rachel had always known she was adopted, but she hadn't known the full truth until she was in her twenties, when she finally got access to her records. That was when she found out about Priscilla, the sister who had been adopted by a rich family, who had grown up in a big house with everything she could ever want. Meanwhile, Rachel had been shuffled from foster home to foster home, never staying in one place long enough to put down roots, never having anyone who really cared about her.

The resentment had started then, festering inside her like a cancer. It only grew worse as the years went by, as she watched Priscilla's life unfold from the sidelines. Every success, every achievement, every smiling photo on social media—it all felt like a slap in the face. That was supposed to be her life. She was the one who should have been living in that big house, married to a handsome, successful man. But instead, she was stuck in this shithole, scraping by with odd jobs and petty crimes just to keep the lights on.

It wasn't fair. None of it was fair.

Rachel flicked the ash from her cigarette onto the floor, her eyes narrowing as she thought about what she had done. She had been planning it for months, ever since she had learned about that trail ride Priscilla was supposed to attend after posting it online. It had taken some doing, but she had found a way to get there, to record that video. And when she watched the final product, she knew she had her sister exactly where she wanted her.

The satisfaction she felt when she sent that DVD to Priscilla's husband was like nothing she had ever experienced. It was like all the years of pain and anger had finally paid off. She could only imagine the look on Priscilla's face when Marcus confronted her, the shock, the fear. It was perfect. And now, it was only a matter of time before everything fell apart for her precious sister.

Rachel crushed the cigarette beneath her boot, a cold smile spreading across her face. She knew it was only the beginning. Priscilla might have had the perfect life up until now, but that was about to change. Rachel was going to tear it all down, piece by piece, until there was nothing left but ruins. She was going to make Priscilla feel every ounce of the pain she had felt, every moment of despair, every second of hopelessness.

And when it was all over, Rachel would finally have what she deserved. She would finally have the life that had been stolen from her.

She grabbed her phone from the cluttered table and scrolled through her contacts until she found the number she was looking for. It was time to take the next step, to push Priscilla even further over the edge. She hit the call button and waited, her heart pounding with anticipation.

"Yo, it's me," she said when the line connected. "I need you to do somethin' for me. You still got that video?"

The voice on the other end was low and gruff. "Yeah, I got it. What you want me to do with it?"

"Leak it to TMZ," Rachel said, her voice dripping with venom. "I want the whole fuckin' world to see it."

There was a pause on the other end, and Rachel could hear the hesitation in the man's voice. "You sure about that? Once it's out there, you can't take it back."

"I don't give a fuck," Rachel snapped. "Just do it. I want to make sure it goes viral. I want that bitch's life to be over."

The man on the other end grunted in acknowledgment. "Aight. Consider it done."

Rachel hung up the phone, a wave of satisfaction washing over her. She could already see the headlines, the social media posts, the news reports. Priscilla was about to become the most infamous woman in the country, and there was nothing she could do to stop it.

As she sat back down on the tattered couch, Rachel allowed herself a moment to savor the victory. She had been waiting for this for so long, had dreamed about it for years. And now, it was finally happening. Priscilla's perfect life was crumbling, and Rachel was the one holding the wrecking ball.

But as the satisfaction faded, a darker feeling began to take its place. It was a feeling Rachel knew all too well, one that had been with her for as long as she could remember. It was the gnawing emptiness that came with knowing that no matter how much she destroyed Priscilla's life, it would never change the fact that her own life was still in ruins. No matter how much she tore down, she would always be stuck in this shithole, alone and forgotten.

She lit another cigarette, trying to push the feeling away, but it lingered, a dark cloud hanging over her. She had spent so many years hating Priscilla, blaming her for everything that had gone wrong in her life, but now that she was finally getting her revenge, it didn't feel as satisfying as she had thought it would. The anger was still there, burning like a fire in her chest, but it was mixed with something else, something she didn't want to acknowledge.

Because deep down, Rachel knew that destroying Priscilla wouldn't make her life any better. It wouldn't erase the years of pain and suffering, the loneliness, the bitterness. It wouldn't bring back the life she had lost, the life she had never had. And it wouldn't fill the void that had been growing inside her for so long.

But she didn't care. She couldn't care. She had come too far, done too much. There was no turning back now. She was going to see this through to the end, no matter what it cost her.

And if it destroyed her along with Priscilla, then so be it.

The next few days passed in a blur, the tension in Rachel's chest growing with each passing hour. She knew the video had been leaked, knew it was only a matter of time before the fallout began. But even as she waited for the world to explode, she couldn't shake the feeling of dread that hung over her like a storm cloud.

She tried to keep herself busy, tried to focus on the next steps, but her mind kept drifting back to Priscilla, to the life she had led, to the life Rachel had always wanted. It wasn't fair. It had never been fair.

But she couldn't stop. She had to see this through. She had to make Priscilla pay for everything she had taken from her, for the life she had stolen.

Chapter 6: The Streets Talk

The streets were buzzing, word spreading faster than wildfire in a dry brush. It didn't take long before everybody and their mama had seen the video—Priscilla Johnson, the so-called Southern belle, caught up in some dirty-ass orgy in a trailer at a trail ride like she was straight outta a cheap porno. The whole thing was scandalous, downright filthy, and folks were eating it up like it was the best gossip they'd ever heard.

In every corner of the city, from the upscale boutiques to the rundown liquor stores, people were talking. Whispers and smirks, side-eyes and snickers, followed Priscilla's name like a bad odor. She went from being the queen of social media, a ranch life goddess with followers who hung on her every word, to being looked at as disloyal gutter trash.

Rachel, meanwhile, was living for it. She had created a mess, a shitstorm that was only getting bigger, and she was loving every second of it. From her cramped, grimy apartment, she watched as Priscilla's perfect little life fell apart online. She kept her ear to the ground, hearing the talk, feeding the flames, making sure the story stayed alive.

"Yo, did you see that video of ol' girl?" one dude said, standing outside a corner store, his voice loud enough for half the block to hear. "Man, I ain't know she got down like that. That shit was wild."

"For real, man," his friend replied, shaking his head with a grin. "She always actin' like she too good for everybody, but look at her now. Ain't nobody gonna wanna touch that no more."

Around the corner, a group of women stood in a tight circle, their voices low but intense. They had all seen the video, all watched Priscilla go from high-class to low-rent in the span of a few minutes. And they were loving it.

"Girl, did you see how she was actin'? Like she ain't got no damn shame," one woman said, her eyes wide with fake shock. "And all this time, she been tryna act like she better than everybody else."

"Please," another woman snorted. "That's what happens when you think you too good for the anybody. The streets will remind your ass real quick who you really are. Humble yo ass real quick."

Rachel soaked it all in, a smug grin on her face as she listened to the chatter. She had been working hard to keep the narrative going, dropping little hints here and there, making sure people stayed interested in the train wreck. She knew how the streets worked, knew how to play the game. And right now, she was winning.

Priscilla, on the other hand, was drowning. Her phone buzzed nonstop with notifications, messages, and calls she didn't want to answer. The comments on her social media were vicious, cruel, a far cry from the adoration she was used to. Her once-loyal followers were turning on her, and it was like watching a pack of wolves tear into a carcass.

"Y'all see this shit? @PriscillaRanchQueen is nothing but a fake ass slut," one comment read, racking up likes and replies faster than Priscilla could keep up.

Another post, this one a meme, showed a picture of Priscilla looking her best, next to a still from the video, her face twisted in ecstasy. The caption read, "From Southern Belle to Gutter Bitch in 3... 2... 1..." The post had gone viral within hours, spreading like poison through the internet.

Priscilla tried to keep up, tried to do damage control, but it was no use. Every attempt to defend herself, to deny the allegations, was met with more ridicule, more scorn. Her sponsors started pulling out, one by one, sending polite but firm messages about how they could no longer associate with her brand. Her followers dropped like flies, unfollowing her in droves, unsubscribing from her channels. Her world was falling apart, and there was nothing she could do to stop it.

In the midst of it all, Marcus was nowhere to be found. He had left the house days ago, after that first confrontation, and hadn't been back since. He wasn't answering her calls, wasn't responding to her texts. It was like he had vanished, leaving Priscilla to face the storm alone.

She felt like she was suffocating, the walls closing in on her with every passing minute. She barely ate, barely slept, her mind consumed with the nightmare her life had become. The perfect world she had spent years building was crumbling around her, and all she could do was watch.

The streets loved a good fall from grace, and Priscilla's was as good as it got. People who had never even heard of her before were talking about her now, her name on everyone's lips, her face plastered across screens and magazine covers. She had become infamous, but for all the wrong reasons.

Rachel reveled in it. She had succeeded beyond her wildest dreams. Priscilla's life was in shambles, and the satisfaction she felt was intoxicating. But even as she celebrated her victory, a part of her felt empty, hollow. The hatred that had fueled her for so long, the anger that had driven her to destroy her sister, was still there, gnawing at her insides.

She had won, but the victory was bittersweet. Because no matter how much she ruined Priscilla's life, it didn't change the fact that her own life was still a mess. She was still stuck in that same shitty apartment, still scraping by, still barely making it. The only difference now was that she had nothing left to aim her anger at, no more targets to destroy.

As the days passed, the scandal only grew. More people came forward with stories about Priscilla, some true, most exaggerated, all damaging. The streets thrived on it, feeding off the drama, the downfall of someone who had once seemed untouchable. The media picked it up, adding fuel to the fire, and soon Priscilla's name was everywhere.

Rachel watched it all unfold with a mix of triumph and despair. She had gotten what she wanted, but it didn't feel like enough. It was like drinking salt water, the more she consumed, the thirstier she became.

The anger, the resentment, it was still there, gnawing at her, demanding more.

The tone of the gossip, the rumors, started to shift. People began asking questions, wondering if there was more to the story. A few brave souls even suggested that maybe, just maybe, Priscilla was telling the truth. That maybe, someone had set her up.

She knew she had to act fast, had to do something to keep the story alive, to keep Priscilla down. But she was running out of ideas, out of time. The satisfaction she had felt just days ago was gone, replaced by a growing sense of dread.

As Rachel sat in her dark apartment, her mind racing, she realized that this was far from over. She had started something she couldn't control, something that was slipping through her fingers like sand. And she knew, deep down, that the worst was yet to come.

Priscilla, meanwhile, was reaching her breaking point. The pressure, the scrutiny, it was too much. She had lost everything—her husband, her career, her reputation. She was a shell of the woman she had once been, and she didn't know how much longer she could hold on.

Chapter 7: Marcus' Betrayal

Marcus was gone more often than not. It had started with him staying out late, claiming he needed space to "clear his head," but Priscilla knew something was off. The man she married used to come home every night, even if it was just to sit in silence after a long day. But now, his absence was a constant, gnawing at her like a sore tooth she couldn't ignore. The tension between them had grown so thick you could cut it with a knife, but Marcus wasn't one to talk things out. He kept his distance, leaving Priscilla to fend for herself in the middle of the mess her life had become.

She tried to reach out to him, to find some semblance of the man she had once known, but every time she tried to get close, he pushed her further away. The distance between them became a canyon, wide and impassable, and no matter how hard she tried, Priscilla couldn't bridge the gap.

Then, one night, she found out why.

Priscilla was at a local bar, one of the few places she could still go without being hounded by reporters or sneered at by strangers. She was nursing a drink, trying to drown out the noise in her head, when she saw them. Marcus, standing in the corner with a young woman pressed up against him, his hands all over her. They were laughing, whispering in each other's ears, oblivious to the world around them.

The woman was half Priscilla's age, a pretty little thing with big eyes and a body that curved in all the right places. She was part of their social circle, one of those hanger-ons who always seemed to be around, even though Priscilla had never paid her much attention. But now, with Marcus's hands on her, she was impossible to ignore.

Priscilla's heart dropped into her stomach as she watched them, her breath catching in her throat. The scene in front of her felt surreal, like a nightmare she couldn't wake up from. She couldn't move, couldn't speak, couldn't do anything but stare as Marcus leaned down to whisper something in the woman's ear, making her giggle like a schoolgirl.

He didn't see Priscilla at first, too wrapped up in his new plaything to notice anything else. But when he did, their eyes locked across the room, and for a moment, Priscilla thought she saw something like guilt flash in his eyes. But it was gone just as quickly, replaced by a look of cold indifference that sent a chill down her spine.

Marcus didn't even have the decency to look ashamed. He just stared at her, his expression hard and unfeeling, like she was the one who had done something wrong. Priscilla's blood boiled, her hands shaking with a mix of anger and betrayal, but she couldn't bring herself to confront him. Not here, not like this.

She turned on her heel and walked out of the bar, her vision blurred by tears she refused to let fall. Her heart felt like it had been ripped out of her chest, stomped on, and thrown in the gutter. She had thought the scandal was the worst thing that could happen to her, but this... this was a whole different level of pain.

When she got home, Priscilla tried to calm herself down, but the images of Marcus with that woman kept playing in her head, over and over again. It felt like a betrayal too deep to comprehend. The man she had loved, the man she had trusted with her heart, had not only abandoned her when she needed him most, but he had replaced her with someone else, someone younger, prettier, and without the baggage of a public scandal.

And the worst part? He didn't even try to hide it.

The next morning, Priscilla woke up to find that Marcus hadn't come home. His side of the bed was untouched, the sheets still neat and tucked in. She sat there in the silence, the reality of her situation crashing down on her like a ton of bricks. Her marriage was over. There was no coming back from this, no fixing what had been broken.

But even as the truth settled in, Priscilla couldn't stop herself from hoping, from wishing that somehow, things could go back to the way they were before. Before the video, before the scandal, before everything had fallen apart. She wanted to believe that Marcus would come to his senses, that he would see what he was doing and realize how much he was hurting her. But deep down, she knew it was a fool's hope.

Days turned into weeks, and Marcus's betrayal became more blatant. He didn't bother to hide his affair, flaunting the other woman like a trophy every chance he got. They showed up at events together, sat in the same circles that Priscilla once occupied, laughing and flirting like they didn't have a care in the world. And the worst part? People accepted it. They whispered behind her back, shot her pitying looks, but no one confronted Marcus. No one told him he was wrong. In their eyes, Priscilla was damaged goods, and Marcus was just moving on.

The humiliation was unbearable. Priscilla felt like she was being suffocated, like the walls were closing in on her and there was no escape. Every time she stepped outside, she felt the weight of their judgment, their scorn, pressing down on her. She couldn't breathe, couldn't think, couldn't function.

Her mind spiraled, the thoughts coming in a jumbled mess that she couldn't control. She started questioning everything—her life, her marriage, her choices. Had she been blind all along? Had Marcus ever really loved her, or had it all been an act? And if it was an act, what did that make her? A fool? A pawn in his game? The questions haunted her, tearing at her already fragile sanity.

Priscilla tried to keep herself together, tried to hold on to some semblance of normalcy, but it was slipping through her fingers like sand. She stopped eating, stopped sleeping, the dark circles under her eyes growing deeper with each passing day. Her once-pristine appearance became disheveled, her clothes wrinkled, her hair unkempt. She didn't recognize the woman in the mirror anymore, the woman who had once been so full of life, so confident and sure of herself.

Now, she was just a shell, empty and broken, barely holding on.

And Marcus? He didn't care. He had moved on, left her behind like she was nothing. The man who had once promised to love her forever had become a stranger, cold and distant, with no regard for the pain he was causing her. He flaunted his new woman, parading her around like a prize he had won, while Priscilla was left to pick up the pieces of her shattered life.

The betrayal cut deep, deeper than Priscilla had ever thought possible. It wasn't just the affair, though that was bad enough. It was the way Marcus had abandoned her, left her to face the fallout of the scandal alone.

Chapter 8: The Twins Reunite

Priscilla stood outside the door of the dingy apartment, her heart pounding like a war drum in her chest. The building reeked of stale cigarettes and desperation, the kind of place you ended up when life had kicked you down so hard you couldn't get back up. She couldn't believe her sister—her twin—was living in this kind of squalor. But there was no turning back now. She had come this far, and she needed answers.

She raised her hand to knock but hesitated. What was she even going to say? She took a deep breath, pushed down the fear, and knocked.

The door creaked open a few inches, and Priscilla found herself staring into a pair of eyes identical to her own. For a moment, it was like looking into a mirror, except this reflection was all wrong—harder, colder, with a bitterness that seemed to seep from every pore.

Rachel's eyes narrowed, her lips curling into a smirk. "Well, well, look who decided to finally show up. The queen herself gracing us peasants with her presence."

"Rachel..." Priscilla's voice wavered, all the anger and pain she had been holding back threatening to spill over. "Can we talk."

"Talk?" Rachel scoffed, pushing the door open wider. "Now you wanna talk? After all this time?"

Priscilla swallowed hard, trying to keep her emotions in check. "Please, just... let me in. We need to sort things out."

Rachel hesitated for a moment, then stepped aside, motioning for Priscilla to enter. The apartment was even worse inside—cramped, dirty, with barely any furniture save for a worn-out couch and a battered coffee table. A roach scuttled across the floor, disappearing into a crack in the wall.

"Nice place," Priscilla said, the words slipping out before she could stop herself.

Rachel laughed, a harsh, grating sound. "Yeah, well, it ain't no ranch, but it's home."

Priscilla stood awkwardly in the middle of the room, unsure of what to do or say. The tension between them was thick, suffocating. Finally, she found her voice.

"Why, Rachel? Why ... I mean are you doing this to me?"

Rachel's eyes flashed with anger. "Why? You really gotta ask that? Look around, Priscilla! Look at what I got, and then think about what you got. You got the life that was supposed to be mine!"

"That's not true," Priscilla shot back, her voice shaking. "We were both adopted. I didn't choose this life any more than you did."

"Bullshit," Rachel snapped, stepping closer, her voice low and venomous. "You think I don't know? You think I didn't do my homework? Your folks picked you, Priscilla. They picked you 'cause you was the pretty one, the sweet one, the one they could show off to their rich-ass friends. And what about me? Where was I? Left to rot in the system, passed around like trash. You stole my life, Priscilla. You stole everything."

Priscilla's heart ached as she listened to Rachel's words, the bitterness, the resentment. "I didn't know, Rachel. I didn't know about you until it was too late. If I had known—"

"If you had known, what?" Rachel interrupted, her eyes blazing. "You woulda saved me? Come on, Priscilla, you ain't no savior. You just like all them other rich bitches, thinkin' you better than everybody else."

Priscilla felt the tears welling up in her eyes, but she blinked them back. She couldn't afford to break down now. "I'm not trying to be better than anyone. I just want to understand. Why did you do it, Rachel? Why did you make that video? Why did you try to destroy my life?"

Rachel sneered, crossing her arms over her chest. "Why? 'Cause it's what you deserve. You got everything handed to you on a silver platter, and what did I get? Nothin'. So yeah, I made that video. I found out about that trail ride you was supposed to go to, and I made sure I was there too. I got with them dudes, recorded the whole thing, and made sure it got to Marcus. And you know what? It worked. Your perfect little life is fallin' apart, just like mine did."

Priscilla felt like the ground had been ripped out from under her. She had suspected, but hearing Rachel say it out loud, hearing the cold, calculated way she had gone about it—it was almost too much to bear.

"Rachel, please," Priscilla whispered, her voice trembling. "I know you're angry, and I understand why. But this... this isn't the way. We're sisters, Rachel. We should be helping each other, not tearing each other apart."

"Sisters?" Rachel spat the word like it was poison. "We ain't sisters, Priscilla. We just happen to share some DNA, that's it. You don't know what it's like, growin' up in the streets, havin' to fight for every scrap, every breath. You had it all handed to you, and you wanna talk about bein' sisters? Please bitch."

Priscilla's heart broke as she listened to Rachel's words, the pain and bitterness that had festered for so long. She wanted to reach out, to bridge the gap between them, but she didn't know how. "I'm sorry, Rachel," she said, her voice barely above a whisper. "I'm sorry for what you went through. But hurting me isn't going to make it better. It's just going to make everything worse."

Rachel's eyes narrowed, her expression hardening. "Maybe. But at least now, you know what it's like to lose everything. At least now, you know what it's like to be me."

Priscilla felt the tears spilling over, running down her cheeks. "I don't want to be your enemy, Rachel. I want to help you. We can start over, try to fix this."

"Fix this?" Rachel laughed, a harsh, bitter sound. "There ain't no fixin' this, Priscilla. This is how it's always been, and this is how it's always gonna be. You got your life, and I got mine. And the sooner you realize that, the better."

Priscilla shook her head, her heart breaking all over again. "I can't accept that, Rachel. I won't."

Rachel stepped closer, her voice low and dangerous. "You don't got a choice, Priscilla. This is the life we got, and you better get used to it. 'Cause I ain't done with you yet."

Priscilla felt a chill run down her spine as she looked into Rachel's eyes, saw the cold, unrelenting hatred there. She realized then that there was nothing she could say, nothing she could do to reach her sister. Rachel was too far gone, too consumed by her anger and bitterness.

Priscilla took a step back, her heart heavy with the weight of everything that had been said. "I'm sorry, Rachel," she said, her voice trembling. "I really am. But I won't let you destroy me. I won't let you win."

Rachel smirked, her eyes glinting with malice. "We'll see about that, sis. We'll see."

Priscilla turned and walked out of the apartment, her heart pounding in her chest. The door slammed shut behind her, the sound echoing in the empty hallway. She felt like she was walking in a nightmare, the world around her spinning out of control.

As she stepped out into the cold night air, Priscilla knew that the fight was far from over. Rachel was determined to destroy her, and she wasn't going to stop until she had taken everything. But Priscilla wasn't going to back down. She couldn't.

She had lost too much already, but she wasn't going to lose herself. Not now, not ever.

The twins had reunited, but the war had only just begun.

Chapter 9: A Web of Lies

Priscilla was barely hanging on. Each day was a new nightmare, and it felt like there was no end in sight. The constant barrage of phone calls, messages, and the never-ending wave of hate online were bad enough. But what made it worse was knowing that it was all part of Ramona's twisted plan. Every lie, every rumor, every piece of dirt being dug up was carefully orchestrated by her sister. And Priscilla was powerless to stop it.

Rachel had made good on her promise. She wasn't done yet.

It started with the media. One day, Priscilla woke up to find her name splashed across the headlines. Stories about her "secret life" were everywhere—tabloids, blogs, even some mainstream news outlets were picking it up. They talked about the video, of course, but now there were new details, new accusations that made Priscilla's head spin.

"Priscilla Johnson: Rodeo Queen or Thief in the Night?"

One particularly nasty article claimed that Priscilla had been involved in a string of thefts at a few trail rides luring and out of town boutiques nearby. The story painted her as a kleptomaniac, a woman who couldn't resist stealing despite her wealth and status. According to the article, she had been quietly paying off victims for years to keep them quiet.

Priscilla knew it was all lies, but the damage was done. The media ate it up, and so did the public. People were quick to believe the worst, and Ramona knew it. She was feeding the beast, and it was tearing Priscilla apart.

Then came the personal attacks. Rachel wasn't content to just ruin Priscilla's public image; she wanted to destroy her personal life too. She started spreading lies to Marcus, feeding him stories that played on his insecurities and his growing mistrust.

"You think you know her, Marcus?" Rachel had said in a recorded phone call that somehow ended up in Marcus's inbox. "You think she's this perfect little wife? Man, Priscilla been playin' you for a fool. I know things 'bout her that would make your skin crawl. She's been cheatin' on you, steal'n from you, and laughin' behind your back the whole time. You just too blind to see it."

Marcus, already on the edge from everything that had happened, snapped. He didn't know who to believe anymore. The woman he had loved, the woman he had married, was starting to look like a stranger. And Rachel's lies were poisoning his mind, making him see betrayal in every look, every word.

One night, Marcus came home drunk, his eyes wild with rage. He had a fistful of printouts in his hand—more stories, more lies. He slammed them down on the table in front of Priscilla, his face twisted with anger.

"Explain this!" he yelled, his voice slurred. "Explain how you've been stealin' from me, how you been lyin' to me all these years!"

Priscilla looked at the papers, her heart sinking. "Marcus, this is all lies. You know me—"

"I don't know shit anymore!" Marcus cut her off, his words sharp as knives. "All I know is that every time I turn around, there's more dirt on you. More shit you been hidin'. How the fuck am I supposed to trust you when all I hear is how you been runnin' around behind my back?"

"Please, Marcus, you gotta believe me," Priscilla pleaded, tears streaming down her face. "This is Rachel. My twin sister. She's doin' this to tear us apart."

"Rachel?" Marcus scoffed. "Your imaginary twin? Come on, Priscilla, you really expect me to buy that bullshit?"

"It's not bullshit!" Priscilla cried, her voice cracking with desperation. "She's real, Marcus. She's real, and she's tryin' to destroy me. I swear, I'm not lyin.'"

But Marcus wasn't listening. He turned away, his hands trembling as he ran them through his hair. "I don't know what to believe anymore," he muttered, his voice filled with despair. "I just... I can't do this. I can't live like this."

Priscilla reached out to him, but he pulled away, his eyes cold and distant. "Marcus, please—"

"No," he said, his voice flat. "I'm done, Priscilla. I'm done with all of this. You need to go."

Priscilla's heart shattered. "What? You're kicking me out?"

Marcus nodded, his expression hardening. "Yeah. I can't have you here no more. Not after everything that's happened. I need you gone."

Priscilla felt like the ground had been ripped out from under her. She couldn't believe what she was hearing. "Where am I supposed to go?"

"I don't care," Marcus said, his voice cold. "Just get out."

Priscilla felt the tears streaming down her face, but there was no point in arguing. She knew Marcus had made up his mind. She turned and walked out of the house, feeling like a ghost as she left behind the life she had known.

With nowhere to go and no one to turn to, Priscilla found herself alone in the streets. She had lost everything—her husband, her home, her reputation. Her friends had abandoned her, too afraid of the fallout to stand by her side. She was completely alone, left to fend for herself in a world that had turned its back on her.

For days, Priscilla wandered the streets from hotel to hotel, her mind numb with shock. She couldn't process what had happened, couldn't understand how her life had fallen apart so quickly. It was like she was living in a nightmare, one she couldn't wake up from.

The few possessions she had managed to grab before leaving the house were stuffed into a small suitcase, which she dragged behind her as she searched for somewhere to stay. But no matter where she went, she couldn't escape the whispers, the stares. People recognized her, and the looks they gave her were filled with judgment, with disdain.

"Hey, ain't that Priscilla Johnson?" she overheard someone say as she passed a group of people on the street. "Yeah, that's her. Heard she been stealin' from folks, lyin' 'bout everything. Can't believe she showed her face 'round here."

Priscilla kept her head down, her heart heavy with shame. She had never felt so small, so worthless. The life she had built, the person she had been, was gone. And in its place was a hollow shell, a woman who had been broken by lies and betrayal.

She found herself at a rundown motel on the edge of town, the kind of place where people went when they had nowhere else to go. The room was small and dirty, with peeling wallpaper and a mattress that sagged in the middle. But it was a roof over her head, and that was all she could ask for.

As she sat on the edge of the bed, staring at the faded carpet, Priscilla felt the weight of everything pressing down on her. She had lost everything, and she didn't know how to get it back. She didn't even know where to start.

Rachel's lies had destroyed her life, and there was no way to fix it. No way to undo the damage that had been done. Priscilla was trapped in a web of lies, and there was no escape.

She would find a way to clear her name, to expose Rachel for the liar she was. And when she did, she would make sure Rachel paid for everything she had done.

As she lay back on the bed, staring up at the cracked ceiling, Priscilla made a silent vow. She would get her life back, no matter what it took. She would find the strength to fight, to rise from the ashes of the life Rachel had burned to the ground.

And when the time came, she would make sure that Rachel felt the full weight of her own lies.

Chapter 10: The Streets Are Watching

The streets had eyes, ears, and long memories. Rachel had always known that. You couldn't move a muscle in the hood without somebody clocking it, and sooner or later, your past would catch up with you. She had been laying low for so long and moving in the shadows. Now she was forgetting that she had made a long list of enemies and wasn't moving under the radar as she had been before. She was always doing dirt, and any wrong move could get her touched so she always had to play it safe and stay put the way. She was out in the open while she was riding high on the destruction of Priscilla's life.

She had played her cards well, or so she thought. Priscilla's fall had been spectacular, a perfect storm of lies, deceit, and revenge. But in her thirst for vengeance, Rachel had forgotten that in the game she was playing, there were no real winners, only survivors. And the streets were starting to remind her of that hard truth.

It started with whispers, low murmurings in the back alleys and corner stores, rumors that Rachel was back on the scene. It wasn't long before those whispers turned into something more concrete, and old faces from her past began emerging from the shadows.

"Yo, you heard 'bout Rachel?" a voice hissed in the darkened corner of a bodega, where the flickering light barely cut through the haze of cigarette smoke. "That bitch think she slick, but folks talkin'. Word is, she robbed the wrong people now she poppin out."

"Man, I thought that chick was locked up or dead," another voice responded, low and cautious. "What she doin' back 'round here?"

"Dunno, but been seen her around, and people ain't happy. She better watch her back."

Rachel could feel the pressure building, the old ghosts of her past beginning to close in. She had burned too many bridges, crossed too many people, and now they were starting to remember. And in the streets, people didn't forget—or forgive.

She knew the stakes, had always known them. But the thrill of seeing Priscilla's world crumble had blinded her to the dangers lurking in her own.

Meanwhile, Priscilla was struggling to survive. Her world had been turned upside down, and the safety net she had once taken for granted was gone. She had no home, no friends, and nowhere to turn. The polished, perfect life she had lived was a distant memory, and in its place was a harsh reality she wasn't prepared for.

With nowhere else to go, she found herself back in the streets—the same streets Rachel had crawled out of. It was a world Priscilla had never known, never understood, and it was a world that didn't give a damn about who you were or what you had. Here, it was all about survival, and Priscilla was woefully unprepared.

She moved through the alleys and side streets like a ghost, trying to avoid the gaze of the people who lived there. But the streets had eyes, and they watched her every move. The whispers followed her too, just like they did Rachel, but these whispers were filled with pity and contempt.

"Yo, ain't that the chick from the videos? What she doin' out here?"

"Damn, she fell off hard. Used to be all over the 'gram, lookin' like she had it all. Now look at her. Look lik she ain't even got a place to stay."

"Shit, that's what happens when you get too high and mighty. The streets'll bring you right back down."

Priscilla heard every word, felt every stare, and each one was like a dagger in her heart. She had always been proud, always held her head high, but now she was nothing. Just another face in the crowd, another casualty of the world she had never understood.

She found refuge in a shelter, a place she never imagined she'd end up. The beds were hard, the rooms cold, and the people there were as broken as she felt. It was a far cry from the life she had known, and the reality of it hit her like a freight train.

Sitting on the edge of a narrow cot, Priscilla stared at the walls, peeling and cracked, the stench of beer from some homeless residents heavy in the air. She felt like she was drowning, and no matter how hard she tried to claw her way out, the darkness was pulling her down.

But even here, in the depths of her despair, the streets were watching. And as the whispers grew louder, Priscilla realized that she wasn't just fighting to survive—she was fighting against a tide that was threatening to sweep her under.

Rachel, meanwhile, was feeling the heat. The people she had crossed in the past were starting to surface, and they weren't happy to see her. Old debts, old grudges—these things didn't just disappear. And now, with her name back on people's lips, those old debts were being called in.

It started small—an old associate, a man named Reggie, catching her off guard outside her apartment. He was a big, burly man with a mean streak, and the look in his eyes told Rachel that he hadn't forgotten the money she owed him for some dope he had given her .

"Rachel," he growled, his voice low and menacing. "You been gone I see ya back huh, girl. Time to pay up."

Rachel tried to play it cool, but inside, her heart was racing. She had known this day would come, but she hadn't expected it to be now, not while she was still basking in the glow of Priscilla's destruction.

"Reggie, man, it ain't like that," she said, trying to keep her voice steady. "I been busy, you know? I got your money, just need a little more time."

Reggie wasn't buying it. He stepped closer, his presence looming over her like a dark cloud. "You think you can fuck around with people like you been doin' I heard you robbed ole dude too You in deep now, girl. Real deep."

Rachel felt a chill run down her spine. She had underestimated just how deep the hole she had dug for herself was. And now, it felt like it was caving in.

But she couldn't let it show. She had to keep up the front, had to make Reggie believe she was still in control. "Look, I got a plan. Big money comin' in. Just give me a few days, and I'll get you what you need."

Reggie stared at her, his eyes cold, calculating. "If ou don't, you gonna find out just how bad things can get."

He turned and walked away, leaving Rachel standing there, her hands trembling. She knew he wasn't bluffing. If she didn't come through, Reggie would come back, and next time, he wouldn't be so polite.

As she watched him disappear into the night, Rachel realized that she was in over her head. The streets felt like they were closing in, and there was no way out. The people she had crossed were circling like vultures, waiting for the moment when she finally slipped, when she was too weak to fight back.

And that moment was coming fast.

Back at the shelter, Priscilla was facing her own battles. The streets weren't just watching her—they were testing her, pushing her to see how far she could go before she broke. Each day was a struggle, each night a fight to keep from being swallowed by the darkness.

She knew she had to be strong, had to find a way to survive. But the streets were relentless, and they didn't care about her past or who she used to be. All they saw was another woman down on her luck, another victim to be chewed up and spit out.

But Priscilla wasn't ready to give up. She wasn't ready to let Rachel win. There was still a part of her that believed she could claw her way back, that she could rise from the ashes and reclaim what was hers.

And as she sat there, staring at the cracks in the walls, she made a decision. She wasn't going to let the streets defeat her. She wasn't going to let Rachel's lies destroy her. She was going to fight back, and she was going to do it on her own terms.

Chapter 11: A Life Unraveled

Priscilla slumped against the thin mattress of the rundown shelter cot, her body heavy with exhaustion. The room was suffocating, its air thick with the smell of mildew and cheap cleaner that couldn't mask the years of grime ground into every surface. The flickering lights cast an eerie, pulsing glow, reminding her of the life she once lived but could no longer touch. The contrast between her past and present was stark—like night and day, like heaven and hell.

The streets had taken her in, chewed her up, and spit her out. She was no longer Priscilla, the Southern belle with the perfect life. She was just another face in the crowd, another soul lost in the dark, twisted world that she had once looked down upon. The irony wasn't lost on her—Rachel had dragged her into this pit, and now she was drowning in it.

She had tried to find work, but she didn't have much experience at anything other than being a wife on social media. And it seemed everywhere she went, they recognized her. The scandal, the rumors—they followed her everywhere, tainting everything she touched. The best she could manage was odd jobs—cleaning filthy motel rooms, washing dishes in grimy back alleys for less than minimum wage. It wasn't enough to live on, barely enough to eat. But it was all she had, and it was slowly killing her.

She had learned quickly that the streets were unforgiving. They didn't care who you were or where you came from. They only cared about survival, and Priscilla was struggling to keep her head above water. The people she encountered weren't the polished, smiling faces she used to know—they were hardened, broken. And they didn't take kindly to outsiders.

She had been mugged twice in the first week, her few remaining dollars ripped from her hands by desperate men who saw her as an easy target. She had begged them to show grace, but it was useless. They took everything—her money, her pride, her sense of safety. She was left with nothing but bruises and a deep, gnawing fear that kept her awake at night.

But the worst part was the terror she felt. The constant, simmering violence that hung in the air around the shelter like a toxic cloud. Fights broke out in the alleys, knives flashing in the dim light as desperate people clashed over scraps. Gunshots rang out in the night, the sounds echoing through the narrow streets like a sinister symphony. Priscilla had learned to keep her head down, to avoid eye contact, to move quickly and quietly through the shadows. But the violence found her anyway, wrapping itself around her like a suffocating shroud.

One night, as she was walking back to the shelter after a long shift at the diner, she found herself cornered by a group of men. Their eyes were dark, hungry, and she knew immediately that they wanted more than just her money. Panic surged through her, but she forced herself to stay calm, to think. She tried to reason with them, to offer them what little she had. But they just laughed, the sound cold and cruel, as they closed in on her.

She fought back, clawing and scratching, using every ounce of strength she had left. But it wasn't enough. They overpowered her, dragging her into a dark alley where nobody would hear her screams. She felt their hands on her, rough and unforgiving, and she knew that this was it. This was the end.

But then, as quickly as it had started, it was over. The men were gone, leaving her bruised and bleeding in the filthy alley. She didn't know why they had left, didn't care. All she knew was that she was still alive, but barely. She dragged herself back to the shelter, her body shaking with pain and fear, and collapsed onto the cot. The darkness and loneliness closed in around her, swallowing her whole.

Rachael wasn't far from these slums, and she kept tabs on Priscilla, making sure to know exactly how far she had fallen. She didn't want to miss a single moment of her sister's suffering. Every time she heard about another setback, another humiliation, she smiled. This was justice, in her eyes. This was what Priscilla deserved for stealing the life that should have been hers.

But even as she enjoyed her sister's misery, a part of Rachel felt empty. The revenge that had once fueled her now felt hollow, unsatisfying. She had destroyed Priscilla, but it hadn't made her life any better. She was still stuck in the same rundown apartment, still scraping by, still alone. The hatred that had driven her was all she had left, and it was consuming her.

She pushed those thoughts aside, focusing instead on the destruction she had wrought. She wasn't done yet. There were still more lies to spread, more damage to do. She had taken everything from Priscilla, but she wanted to make sure there was nothing left, no hope, no chance of recovery.

As Priscilla lay on the shelter cot, staring up at the cracked ceiling, she felt like she was sinking into a pit of despair. The life she had known was gone, and she didn't know how to get it back. She didn't even know if she wanted to. The streets had broken her, taken everything from her, and she didn't have the strength to fight back anymore.

But as the days passed, something inside her began to shift. The pain, the fear, the despair—they were still there, but beneath them, something else was starting to grow. A spark of anger, a flicker of determination. She had been pushed to the brink, but she wasn't ready to give up yet. Not completely.

Priscilla wasn't the same woman she had been before. The streets had changed her, hardened her. She wasn't just fighting to survive anymore—she was fighting to reclaim her life, to take back what had been stolen from her.

As she stared out the shelter window, watching the neon lights flicker in the darkness, Priscilla made a vow. She would rise from the ashes of her old life. She would find a way to get back on her feet, to take back control. And when the time came, she would make sure that Ramona paid for everything she had done.

The streets had taken everything from her, but they had also given her something in return—a new sense of purpose, a new fire burning inside her. Priscilla was down, but she wasn't out.

And as she plotted her next move, she knew one thing for sure—Rachels victory was about to be short-lived. The real fight was just beginning.

Chapter 12: The Truth Begins to Surface

Priscilla sat in the dimly lit corner of a run-down diner, her eyes bloodshot from lack of sleep. The place smelled like burnt coffee and grease, but it was quiet, a rare commodity in the world she was now forced to navigate. Her hands trembled slightly as she flipped through the old documents in front of her, papers she had managed to pry loose from her adoption records. The truth was starting to unravel, and it was darker than she had ever imagined.

She had always known that she was adopted, but she never questioned it. Why would she? She had grown up in a loving home, with parents who had given her everything she could ever want. But now, as she pieced together the fragmented story of her past, she realized that the life she had taken for granted was built on lies.

The papers she held were yellowed with age, the ink faded in places, but the words were clear enough. Her adoption wasn't the clean-cut story she had always believed. There were gaps, inconsistencies, things that didn't add up. And the more she dug, the more she found.

Priscilla's heart pounded as she read through the documents again, her mind racing. There was something here, something big. She could feel it in her bones. This wasn't just about jealousy, about Rachel being angry that she had a better life. There was something deeper, something that had been buried for years.

She had started to uncover the truth. A woman at the shelter had mentioned a lawyer who used to handle shady adoption cases back in the day. The name had stuck with Priscilla, gnawing at the back of her mind until she finally decided to look into it. That's when she found the first crack in the story she had been told all her life.

The lawyer, now old and retired, had been involved in all sorts of crooked dealings—illegal adoptions, baby trafficking, forging documents to cover up his tracks. Priscilla's stomach churned as she realized that she might be part of one of those shady deals. Her adoption papers, which she had never thought to question, suddenly seemed suspect.

But it wasn't just the lawyer that bothered her. As she dug deeper, she found references to another name, one she hadn't expected—Rachel's. It was buried deep in the files, almost as if someone had tried to erase it. But it was there, a connection she couldn't ignore.

Priscilla's mind raced with possibilities. What if their separation wasn't an accident? What if someone had deliberately kept them apart, manipulated their lives for reasons she couldn't yet understand? And why had Rachel's name been hidden, almost as if someone didn't want the two sisters to find each other?

The questions gnawed at her, but there were no easy answers. The more she uncovered, the more tangled the web became. It was like peeling back the layers of an onion, each revelation more painful than the last.

She knew she had to confront Rachel, but this time it wasn't just about the lies and the betrayal. It was about finding the truth, no matter how dark it might be. There was something here, something that had been hidden from both of them, and Priscilla was determined to uncover it.

But Rachel wasn't going to make it easy. Priscilla knew that her sister was still out there, lurking in the shadows, waiting for her next move. The thought of facing her again sent a chill down Priscilla's spine, but she pushed the fear aside. She couldn't back down now. She had to know the truth.

As Priscilla stared at the documents in front of her, a sense of urgency gripped her. Time was running out. If she didn't act soon, she might lose the chance to uncover the truth. And she knew, deep down, that this truth was the key to everything—to understanding Rachel's hatred, to reclaiming her life, to finally finding some measure of peace.

She grabbed her phone and dialed a number. The line rang several times before a gruff voice answered. "Yeah?"

"Hi my name is Priscilla," she said, her voice steady despite the fear gnawing at her insides. "I need to talk to you."

There was a pause on the other end, then a low chuckle. "What you want, girl?"

"I need information," Priscilla replied, her tone firm. "I need to know everything about my adoption. I have some questions. There's something going on, something bigger. And I want to know what it is."

The man on the other end hesitated, then sighed. "Aight. Meet me at 3628 Grainger Street."

"I'll be there," she said, ending the call.

Priscilla's heart raced as she grabbed her coat and headed out the door. The streets were dark, the air thick with the scent of rain and decay. She moved quickly, her mind focused on the task at hand. She knew the man she was meeting was dangerous, but he was also the only one who could give her the answers she needed.

As she walked through the narrow, grimy streets, the weight of what she was about to uncover pressed down on her. The truth was out there, just beyond her reach, and it was calling to her, pulling her deeper into the darkness.

She arrived at the meeting spot—a rundown warehouse on the edge of town. The place was abandoned, its windows shattered, the walls covered in graffiti. It was the kind of place where deals were made in the shadows, where secrets were exchanged for a price.

The man was waiting for her inside, leaning against a rusted metal beam. His face was hidden in the shadows, but Priscilla recognized his voice when he spoke.

"Didn't think you would show up here," he said, his tone mocking.

Priscilla stepped closer, her eyes narrowing. "I'm not here to play games. I want the truth."

The man chuckled, the sound low and menacing. "You want the truth? You sure 'bout that? 'Cause once you hear it, there ain't no goin' back."

"I don't care," Priscilla replied, her voice steady. "I need to know what happened, why my sister Rachel hates me so much. I need to know the truth about our adoption."

The man stepped out of the shadows, revealing a face scarred by years of hard living. He looked at Priscilla with a mix of curiosity and pity. "You don't get it, do you? This ain't just 'bout you and Rachel. This goes way deeper than that. Your adoption, it wasn't no accident. It was a setup from the start."

Priscilla's heart skipped a beat. "What do you mean?"

The man sighed, running a hand through his graying hair. "Your parents, they wanted a kid, but they didn't want no baggage. So they paid to have you, clean and legal. But Rachel was the baggage they didn't want."

Priscilla's blood ran cold. "You're lying."

"I wish I was," the man replied, his voice grim. "But it's the truth. Rachel was supposed to disappear, but it seems like she didn't."

Priscilla felt like the ground was crumbling beneath her. The life she had known, the family she had loved, it was all built on a lie. And Rachel's hatred, her desire for revenge, it all made sense now. They had both been victims, both been played.

But the truth didn't bring relief—it brought a new kind of pain. And as Priscilla stood there, staring at the man who had just shattered her world, she knew that this was only the beginning. The truth was out, but the consequences were still unfolding.

She had to confront Rachel, had to face her sister with this new knowledge. But she knew it wouldn't be easy. Ramona's hatred was deep, and the truth alone might not be enough to heal the wounds that had festered for so long.

As Priscilla left the warehouse, the weight of the truth pressing down on her, she felt a new sense of urgency. The past was catching up with them both, and there was no escaping it now. The truth had begun to surface, and it was pulling them both into the darkness.

Chapter 13: The Secret Unveiled

Priscilla sat on the floor of the grimy shelter, her back pressed against the cold wall, staring at the pile of papers spread out in front of her. The documents, old and yellowed, told a story she never could have imagined. A story that made her stomach churn and her heart feel like it was being torn apart. She had uncovered the truth, but it was far more twisted than she could have ever prepared for.

Her hands trembled as she picked up a particularly damning piece of paper—a birth certificate. It listed the names of her and Rachel's biological mother, but the details scrawled in the margins, notes from a social worker, revealed a dark secret. Their mother had been involved in some shady, illegal activities. The kind that ruined lives and destroyed families. Priscilla's mind raced as she tried to process the revelation that their mother had been a junkie, caught up in a vicious cycle of addiction and crime.

But the worst part was what the documents revealed about their separation. Priscilla and Rachel hadn't been split up by some tragic accident or a simple adoption agency mix-up. No, it was much more sinister than that. Their biological mother had sold one of them—sold Rachel—to fund her drug habit. Priscilla's adoptive parents had paid for a clean slate, a fresh start with just one child, and Rachel was thrown away. She had been abandoned, discarded like trash, while Priscilla was given a life of luxury and love.

The weight of the truth hit Priscilla like a sledgehammer, knocking the breath out of her lungs. She could hardly believe what she was reading, but the pieces all fit together too well to be anything but the ugly truth. Their mother had chosen her addiction over her daughters, and Rachel had paid the ultimate price.

Priscilla's heart broke as she imagined what her sister must have gone through, growing up knowing that she had been the one left behind. It explained everything—Rachel's hatred, her need for revenge, her bitterness. Rachel wasn't just angry; she was broken, scarred by a lifetime of abandonment and betrayal. And now, Priscilla understood why.

She could almost hear Rachel's voice, filled with that familiar mix of anger and pain, echoing in her head. "You think I'm just jealous, huh? That I just wanted your fancy life, your pretty little house? Nah, it's deeper than that. I hate you because you got away. You got the life that was supposed to be mine, while I got left in the gutter."

Tears welled up in Priscilla's eyes as she clutched the papers to her chest. She had known that their lives had taken different paths, but she had never known the full extent of the tragedy that had shaped Rachel's life. The knowledge that her sister's suffering had been the result of their mother's actions, and that Priscilla had been spared simply by chance, was almost too much to bear.

Priscilla's mind raced, replaying every interaction she had ever had with Rachel, every fight, every harsh word. She had been so focused on protecting herself, on defending her own life, that she hadn't taken the time to truly understand where Rachel was coming from. Now, with the truth laid bare in front of her, she felt a deep sense of guilt and sorrow.

How could she have been so blind? How could she have not seen the pain that was driving Rachel, the agony that had been festering inside her for years? Priscilla had always been the one who got away, the one who lived in a bubble of privilege and comfort, while Ramona had been left to fend for herself in a world that showed her no mercy.

Priscilla wiped the tears from her eyes, trying to regain her composure. She knew she had to confront Rachel with this new information, but she also knew it wouldn't be easy. Rachel's hatred ran deep, and the truth, while shocking, might not be enough to heal the wounds that had been inflicted so long ago.

But Priscilla had to try. She couldn't let this revelation go unanswered. She had to face Rachel, to tell her what she had discovered, and to finally understand the full extent of the pain that had driven her sister to such desperate actions.

With a heavy heart, Priscilla gathered the papers and stuffed them into her bag. The shelter felt even more suffocating now, the walls closing in on her as she prepared to confront the reality of her family's dark past. She knew this conversation would be one of the hardest of her life, but she also knew it was necessary. The truth had to come out, no matter how painful it might be.

She left the shelter and made her way through the streets, the air thick with the sounds of the city. It was late, and the streets were filled with the usual mix of danger and despair. Priscilla kept her head down, trying to block out the noise and focus on what she had to do.

Finally, she reached the building where Rachel was staying. It was a run-down apartments, the kind of place that reeked of desperation and decay. Priscilla hesitated for a moment, her heart pounding in her chest, before steeling herself and pushing through the front door.

The hallway was dimly lit, the flickering lights casting eerie shadows on the cracked walls. Priscilla walked slowly, her footsteps echoing in the silence, until she reached Ramona's door. She took a deep breath and knocked.

The door creaked open, and Rachel stood there, her expression cold and guarded. She looked Priscilla up and down, her eyes narrowing. "What the hell you doin' here?"

Priscilla swallowed hard, trying to find the right words. "We need to talk, Rachel. There's something you need to know. Something I just found out."

Rachel crossed her arms, her face hardening. "I don't got nothin' to say to you, Priscilla. You should go back to your fancy-ass world and leave me the fuck alone."

"I know what our mother did," Priscilla said, her voice trembling but determined. "I know she sold you to fund her addiction. I know she abandoned you."

Rachel's eyes flashed with anger, but there was something else there too—pain, buried deep but still very much alive. She stared at Priscilla, her hands clenched into fists. "So what? You think tellin' me what I already know is gonna change anything? You think it's gonna make up for all the shit I been through?"

Priscilla shook her head, her heart breaking for her sister. "No, it's not. But I need you to know that I didn't know, Rachel. I didn't know any of this until now. I didn't know what our mother did, or why you've hated me so much. But I understand now, and I'm sorry. I'm so, so sorry."

Rachel's face twisted with emotion, a mixture of rage and sorrow. She took a step back, shaking her head. "Sorry? You think sorry is gonna fix this? You think it's gonna make up for all the years I spent wonderin' why she didn't want me, why you got the life I was supposed to have?"

Priscilla felt tears welling up again, but she forced herself to stay strong. "No, it won't. But maybe it can be a start. Maybe we can find a way to move forward, together."

Rachel stared at her, her eyes hard, but there was a flicker of something else—something that Priscilla couldn't quite place. She opened her mouth to speak, but then closed it again, the words dying in her throat. Finally, she shook her head, her voice low and bitter. "You don't get it, Priscilla. You never will. You got no idea what it's like to grow up knowin' you ain't wanted, knowin' you were sold like you was nothin'. You got no idea what that does to a person."

Priscilla took a step forward, her voice soft but insistent. "Then help me understand, Rachel. Help me understand what you've been through, so we can figure this out together."

Rachel looked at her for a long moment, her eyes filled with pain and uncertainty. But then, just as quickly, the hardness returned. She took a step back, her face shutting down. "Ain't nothin' to figure out. You got your life, and I got mine. We done here."

Priscilla's heart sank as she watched Rachel turn away, retreating back into the darkness of her apartment. The door closed with a final, resounding thud, leaving Priscilla standing alone in the dim hallway, her heart heavy with the weight of everything she had learned.

She had uncovered the truth, but it had only deepened the chasm between them. And as she stood there, the reality of their situation settling in, Priscilla knew that the road ahead was going to be even harder than she had imagined. The truth had been unveiled, but the battle was far from over.

And in the depths of her soul, Priscilla felt a growing sense of determination. She wasn't going to give up on her sister, not now, not ever. She would find a way to break through Ramona's walls, to reach the person she knew was still in there, buried beneath all the pain and anger. But it would take time, and it would take everything she had.

The truth had been uncovered, but the journey had only just begun.

Chapter 14: Rachel's Downfall

Rachel was slipping. She could feel it, like the ground was crumbling beneath her feet, and no matter how hard she tried to hold on, she was sliding down into a pit she'd spent her whole life trying to escape. The streets were closing in on her, the walls tightening, and the life she thought she had control over was spiraling out of it fast.

The people she had crossed over the years, the ones she had thought she was hiding from, were suddenly everywhere. They were the ghosts from her past, lurking in the shadows, waiting for the right moment to remind her that she wasn't untouchable. She had made too many enemies, burned too many bridges, and now the flames were licking at her heels.

It started with Reggie. She had seen him around, felt his eyes on her like a predator stalking prey. He wasn't one to let things go, and she knew she had fucked him over bad enough that he wouldn't rest until he got what he was owed. She tried to avoid him, keeping to the back streets, moving quietly, but Reggie had a way of finding people. He wasn't just looking for payback; he was looking to send a message. And Rachel was beginning to realize that she was the message.

One night, she was on her way back to her apartment, the cold wind biting through her thin jacket, when she felt a presence behind her. She quickened her pace, her heart pounding, but it was no use. She turned a corner, and there he was—Reggie, flanked by two of his boys, blocking her path.

"Rachel," Reggie said, his voice low and menacing. "You been dodgin' me. But I told you, I don't forget."

Rachel tried to keep her cool, but she could feel the fear creeping up her spine. She had been in tight spots before, but this felt different.

There was a finality to Reggie's tone that made her stomach churn. "Reggie, man, we can work this out. I just need a little more time."

Reggie laughed, but it wasn't a pleasant sound. It was cold, sharp, like a knife sliding against bone. "Time's up, Ramona. You think you can keep playin' games, but this ain't no game. I been patient long enough."

The two men flanking Reggie stepped forward, and Rachel felt her heart seize in her chest. She knew what was coming, knew that talking her way out wasn't an option this time. They weren't here to negotiate. They were here to collect.

Before she could react, one of the men grabbed her by the arm, yanking her into the alley. She struggled, tried to fight back, but it was no use. They were too strong, too fast, and she was too worn out from the constant running, the fear that had been eating away at her.

Reggie stepped closer, his eyes cold as he looked down at her. "This is what happens when you fuck with people, Rachel. You think you're smart, think you can play everyone you definitely can't play me bitch."

He nodded to his boys, and the beating began. Fists rained down on her, heavy and brutal, each one driving the air from her lungs, each one a reminder that she wasn't invincible. She tried to scream, but the pain was too much, her voice choked off by the blows that kept coming, relentless and unforgiving.

When they finally stopped, she was curled up on the ground, blood dripping from her mouth, her body aching from the onslaught. Reggie crouched down next to her, his voice low, almost gentle. "This is just the beginning, girl. You got more to pay, and I'm gonna make sure you do."

With that, he stood up, leaving her lying in the filthy alley, broken and bleeding. Rachel lay there for what felt like hours, the world spinning around her, her mind struggling to process what had just happened. She had thought she was untouchable; thought she could play the game and win. But now, as she lay there, she realized how wrong she had been.

It took all the strength she had left to drag herself up from the ground, her body screaming in protest with every movement. She stumbled back to her apartment, barely making it through the door before collapsing on the floor. The pain was overwhelming, but even worse was the realization that she was alone. She had pushed everyone away, and now, when she needed help the most, there was no one to turn to.

The days blurred together as Rachel tried to recover, tried to figure out what to do next. She knew Reggie wasn't done with her, knew that the streets wouldn't let her slip away so easily. She was marked now, a target, and there was no escaping it.

But as she lay in her apartment, nursing her wounds, another thought crept into her mind. A thought that filled her with dread, but also with a strange sense of clarity. She had spent so long blaming Priscilla, hating her for the life she had, that she had never stopped to think about who was really responsible for her pain. It wasn't just Priscilla—it was their mother, the woman who had sold her for a fix, who had abandoned her to a life of misery.

The truth had been there all along, but Rachel had been too blinded by her anger to see it. And now, as her life unraveled around her, she couldn't escape it. The real enemy wasn't Priscilla. It was the woman who had brought them into this world and then left them to fend for themselves.

But it was too late for that now. The damage had been done, and there was no going back. Rachel had burned too many bridges, made too many enemies. The streets were closing in on her, and she didn't know how much longer she could keep running.

As the days turned into nights, and the nights into days, Rachel felt the walls closing in tighter and tighter. The streets were watching, waiting for her to make a mistake, to slip up just once. And when she did, they would be there, ready to take her down for good.

The desperation grew, a gnawing fear that kept her awake at night, that made every shadow seem like a threat. She knew she couldn't keep going like this, but she didn't know how to stop. The life she had built, the life she had thought was so secure, was crumbling around her, and she was powerless to stop it.

Rachel's downfall had begun, and there was no way out. The streets had claimed her, and they weren't letting go. Not this time.

Chapter 15: Priscilla Fights Back

Priscilla stood in front of the cracked mirror in the dingy shelter bathroom, staring at her reflection. The woman looking back at her was not the same one who had once lived a life of luxury and ease. This woman had been through hell and back, beaten down by the streets, betrayed by those she loved, and left with nothing. But despite the bruises, despite the scars, there was something new in her eyes—a fire that hadn't been there before.

She had spent too long wallowing in the pain, letting Rachels's hatred consume her, but that was over now. She knew the truth, and with it came a strength she hadn't realized she possessed. The knowledge that their mother had sold Rachel, had abandoned her to a life of suffering, had shaken Priscilla to her core. But it had also given her a purpose. She wasn't just fighting for herself anymore; she was fighting for the sister who had been lost to the streets.

Priscilla took a deep breath, her mind racing as she thought about her next move. She couldn't do this alone; she needed allies, people who knew the game as well as Rachel did. People who could help her take back control of her life.

The first person she thought of was Keisha, her old friend from back in the day. They hadn't talked in a while, not since Priscilla's life had spiraled out of control, but Keisha was loyal, and she knew the streets. If anyone could help her, it was Keisha.

Priscilla grabbed her phone and dialed Keisha's number, her heart pounding as she waited for her to pick up. After a few rings, she heard a familiar voice on the other end.

"Priscilla? Damn, girl, where you been? I been worried 'bout you."

Priscilla felt a surge of relief wash over her. "Keisha, I need your help."

There was a pause on the other end, then Keisha's voice hardened. "You know I got your back, Priscilla, always have."

Priscilla quickly filled her in on everything that had happened—the truth about their mother, Rachel's attacks, and her determination to fight back. Keisha listened in silence, and when Priscilla was done, she didn't hesitate.

"Aight, we gon' handle this," Keisha said, her voice firm. "Rachel don't know who she messin' with. You ain't alone in this, Priscilla. We gon' get this bitch, but we gotta be smart 'bout it."

Priscilla felt a weight lift off her shoulders. She wasn't alone anymore. With Keisha by her side, she knew they had a fighting chance.

Over the next few days, Priscilla and Keisha began to put their plan into motion. Keisha tapped into her network, reaching out to people who could connect her with the right people, people who were willing to help. They gathered information, piecing together the full extent of Rachel's schemes, and started to stack evidence.

Priscilla was relentless. She went after Rachel's weak spots, using the knowledge she had gained to her advantage. She knew Rachel's past, knew the people she had crossed, and she wasn't afraid to use that information. She started making calls, setting up meetings, using every resource at her disposal to turn the tide in her favor.

She reconnected with old allies, people who had once been part of her life before everything fell apart. Some were hesitant at first, but once they heard the full story, they came around. They saw the fire in Priscilla's eyes, the determination in her voice, and they knew she was serious. This wasn't the same Priscilla they had known before. This was a woman who had been pushed to the edge and was ready to fight her way back.

As Priscilla gathered her forces, Rachel was beginning to feel the pressure. The people she had thought she could trust were starting to turn on her, spooked by the rumors that were circulating, the whispers that Priscilla was coming for her. Rachel had always been good at playing the game, but now, the game was playing her.

She tried to keep up appearances, tried to act like she was still in control, but the cracks were starting to show. The streets were talking, and what they were saying wasn't good.

She lashed out, trying to keep control, but it was no use. The harder she pushed, the more she lost. And as the walls started to close in, she realized that her revenge had cost her more than she could have ever imagined.

Priscilla, on the other hand, was gaining momentum. She had a fire inside her now, a determination that drove her forward, even when things got tough. She knew she was on the right path, and she wasn't going to stop until Rachel was brought down.

The conflict between the sisters was reaching a boiling point. Every move Priscilla made pushed Rachel further into a corner, and every move Rachel made only strengthened Priscilla's resolve. The tension between them was palpable, like a coiled spring ready to snap.

One night, as Priscilla was leaving a meeting with one of her new allies, she felt the hairs on the back of her neck stand up. She turned, her eyes scanning the darkened street, and saw a figure lurking in the shadows. It was Rachel.

For a moment, they just stared at each other, the air between them thick with tension. Then Rachel stepped forward, her face twisted with anger and fear.

"You think you can come into my world and play my game? You don't know nothin' 'bout the streets. You don't know nothin' 'bout me."

Priscilla stood her ground, her heart pounding in her chest. "I know enough, Rachel. I know what you did to me, what you've done to other people. And I know that it ends now."

Rachel's eyes narrowed, her fists clenched at her sides. "You think you can stop me? I been fightin' all my life, Priscilla. You just now learnin' what it's like to survive. But I been doin' this since day one. You ain't got what it takes."

Priscilla felt a surge of anger rise up inside her. "Maybe I didn't before, but I do now. I've been through hell, Rachel, and I'm still standin'. I ain't afraid of you anymore. You wanna fight? Then let's fight. But I'm tellin' you right now, I'm not backin' down."

The two sisters stood there, the tension crackling in the air like electricity. It was a standoff, a moment that felt like it could explode into violence at any second. But then, just as quickly as it had flared up, Rachel backed down.

She took a step back, her eyes still locked on Priscilla's. "This ain't over," she hissed, before turning and disappearing into the shadows.

Priscilla watched her go, her heart still racing. She knew Rachel wasn't bluffing, knew that the fight was far from over. But for the first time in a long time, she felt like she had the upper hand.

The tide was turning, and Priscilla was ready to take back everything that had been stolen from her. She was fighting for her own future, a future that was finally within her reach.

As she walked away, the city lights flickering above her, Priscilla knew that the final showdown was coming. The battle between the sisters was about to reach its climax, and when it did, there would be no turning back.

Chapter 16: The Confrontation

The night was thick with tension, the air heavy with the threat of violence. The city's lights flickered in the distance, but here, in the forgotten corners of the streets, shadows reigned. Priscilla stood in the middle of the empty warehouse, her heart pounding in her chest. This was it—the moment everything had been leading up to. The final confrontation with Rachel.

She had called Rachel to meet her here, the place where it had all begun, where their lives had first been torn apart by secrets and lies. The cold concrete under her feet, the echo of every sound—it all felt like the setting for a fight to the death. And maybe that's what it was. Only one of them was walking out of here with their life intact.

The door creaked open, and Rachel stepped inside, her silhouette sharp against the dim light filtering through the dirty windows. Her face was set in a hard mask, but there was something in her eyes—something dark and dangerous. She was ready for a fight, and Priscilla knew she had to be, too.

Rachel walked slowly toward her, each step deliberate, her hands clenched into fists at her sides. "You really think you can stand here and talk your way outta this, Priscilla? After everything you done?"

Priscilla's jaw tightened, the anger she had been holding back for so long bubbling to the surface. "This ain't about talkin', Rachel. This is about endin' this, once and for all. We ain't got nothin' left to lose."

Rachel's lips twisted into a sneer. "You got that right. But you don't understand, Priscilla. You ain't never understood. This ain't just about what you did, or what our mama did. This is about the life I had to live 'cause you got to walk away. You got to live like a queen while I was out here fightin' to survive."

Priscilla felt the sting of those words, but she pushed the pain aside. "I didn't know, Rachel! I didn't know what happened to you, or why. But I know now. And I'm not here to fight you—I'm here to stop this."

Rachel laughed, the sound bitter and cold. "Stop it? You think you can stop this? It's too late for that, sis."

Priscilla took a step forward, her voice shaking with emotion. "It doesn't have to be like this. We can walk away, Rachel. We can leave all this behind."

Rachel's eyes narrowed, her anger flaring. "You still don't get it! You can't just walk away from the streets, Priscilla. You can't just decide to leave when things get too hard. This is my life. This is all I got."

Priscilla felt her heart break for her sister, but she knew there was no turning back now. The tension between them had been building for too long, and there was only one way this was going to end. "Then I guess we gotta do this."

Rachel's eyes flashed with fury, and before Priscilla could react, she lunged forward, her fist swinging with all the force of years of pent-up rage. Priscilla barely managed to dodge the blow, stumbling back as Rachel came at her again, her fists flying.

The fight was brutal, raw, and primal. There was no finesse, no strategy—just two women fighting with everything they had, each blow landing with the weight of their shared history. Rachel was fast, driven by a lifetime of anger and pain, but Priscilla had learned to fight, too. She had been broken down, humiliated, and left with nothing, but she had come out stronger, more determined.

They crashed into each other, fists and elbows striking flesh, the sound of their struggle echoing through the empty warehouse. Priscilla felt the sting of Ramona's knuckles against her cheek, tasted blood as her lip split open. But she didn't back down. She couldn't.

"Why'd you have to hate me so much?" Priscilla yelled, her voice raw with pain and desperation. "Why couldn't you see that we coulda been in this together?"

Rachel's answer was another vicious punch, this one aimed straight at Priscilla's gut. "You never wanted me, Priscilla! You never looked for me! You got your perfect life, and you left me to rot!"

Priscilla gasped for breath, but she didn't fall. She grabbed Rachel by the shoulders and shoved her back, her eyes blazing with a mix of anger and sorrow. "I was just a kid! I didn't know! But you—you let that hate eat you alive!"

They struggled against each other, bodies slamming into walls, knocking over old crates and debris. The pain was excruciating, but it fueled them both, drove them to keep going, to keep fighting. It was as if all the years of pain, betrayal, and anger had been leading to this one moment, and neither of them was willing to back down.

Rachel's breath came in ragged gasps as she circled Priscilla, her eyes wild. "You always had it so easy, Priscilla. Everything just handed to you. But I had to fight for everything I got. I had to claw my way up from the gutter, and you think I'm just gonna let you walk away now?"

Priscilla wiped the blood from her mouth, her voice shaking with determination. "I never had it easy, Rachel. I had my own battles. But I'm not here to prove nothin'. I'm here to stop this madness before it destroys us both."

But Rachel wasn't listening. She charged at Priscilla again, her fists swinging, her face twisted with fury. Priscilla blocked the first punch, but the second one caught her off guard, sending her stumbling back into a stack of crates. The wood splintered under the impact, and she collapsed to the ground, dazed.

Rachel stood over her, breathing heavily, her fists still clenched. For a moment, it seemed like she was going to finish it, but something in Priscilla's eyes made her hesitate.

"You ain't me, Priscilla," Rachel said, her voice cracking. "You don't know what it's like to grow up knowin' you were the one left behind. You don't know what that does to a person."

Priscilla looked up at her sister, her vision blurred with tears. "I know now, Rachel. And I'm sorry. I'm sorry for everything you went through. But killin' me won't make it right. It won't bring you peace."

Rachel's expression faltered, the anger in her eyes dimming just a little. For the first time, she looked uncertain, like the weight of her actions was finally crashing down on her. She backed away, her hands trembling.

But the streets had hardened Rachel, and in the end, that hardness won out. She shook her head, her face hardening again. "You don't get it, Priscilla. It's too late for sorry. It's too late for all of this."

She turned away, walking toward the door, leaving Priscilla lying on the cold concrete floor. But just as she reached the exit, Priscilla's voice stopped her in her tracks.

"It ain't too late for us, Rachel. It ain't too late to stop this."

Rachel froze, her back to Priscilla, her shoulders tense. The silence stretched between them, heavy with everything that had been left unsaid. Then, without turning around, Rachel spoke, her voice low and filled with a sorrow that cut through the darkness.

"You think you can save me, Priscilla? You think you can fix all this?"

Priscilla struggled to her feet, every muscle in her body aching. "Maybe not. But we can try. We can start over."

Rachel stood there for a long moment, her fists clenched at her sides. Then, slowly, she turned to face Priscilla. The anger was still there, but it was tempered now, softened by something else—something that looked a lot like hope.

For a moment, it seemed like they might actually find a way out of the darkness, a way to heal the wounds that had been festering for so long. But the streets had other plans.

A loud bang echoed through the warehouse, and Priscilla's eyes widened in shock as she saw the flash of a gun in Rachels hand. The pain hit her like a freight train, a burning sensation in her side that made her gasp for air. She looked down, saw the blood spreading across her shirt, and fell to her knees.

Rachel's eyes widened in horror as she realized what she had done. She dropped the gun, her hands shaking as she rushed to Priscilla's side. "No... no, no, no... I didn't mean to... I didn't..."

Priscilla looked up at her, her vision fading. "Rachel..."

But before she could say anything else, the world went black.

Rachel knelt beside her sister, tears streaming down her face, her hands stained with Priscilla's blood.

Chapter 17: Aftermath and Betrayal

The hospital room was quiet except for the steady beep of the heart monitor. Priscilla lay in the bed, her body battered and bruised, a bandage wrapped tightly around her side where the bullet had torn through her flesh. The room was dim, the only light coming from the small lamp on the bedside table, casting long shadows on the walls. It had been days since the confrontation with Rachel, and while the physical wounds were healing, the emotional scars were far deeper, far more painful.

Priscilla stared at the ceiling, her mind replaying the events over and over, like a broken record she couldn't stop. She had come so close to ending the cycle of hatred, to finding some semblance of peace with her sister. But in the end, the streets and the street life her sister had chose had claimed her as another victim, and she was left to pick up the pieces of a life shattered beyond recognition.

She winced as she shifted in bed, the pain a constant reminder of how close she had come to losing her life. But the physical pain was nothing compared to the ache in her heart, the deep, gnawing sense of betrayal that Marcus's actions had left behind and the hatred her own flesh and blood had for her.

The door to her room creaked open, and Keisha stepped inside, her expression grim. She had been Priscilla's lifeline through all of this, the one person who hadn't abandoned her, even when the rest of the world had turned its back. Keisha pulled up a chair beside the bed and sat down, her eyes filled with concern.

"How you feelin', girl?" Keisha asked, her voice soft but laced with the raw edge of the streets they both knew too well.

Priscilla shrugged, wincing at the pain the movement caused. "I'm alive, I guess. Ain't sure how I feel 'bout that yet."

Keisha nodded, her gaze dropping to the floor. "They got Rachel. She's in custody. Cops say she'll be goin' away for a long time."

Priscilla felt a mix of emotions at the news—relief, sadness, and a deep, aching sorrow that her sister's life had come to this. "She didn't mean to shoot me, Keisha. I know she didn't."

"Maybe," Keisha replied, her tone flat. "But she did. And now she gotta face the consequences. Ain't no runnin' from it."

Priscilla closed her eyes, the weight of everything pressing down on her like a ton of bricks. She had wanted so badly to save Rachel, to pull her out of the darkness that had consumed her. But in the end, it had been too much, and now they were both paying the price.

"Marcus," Priscilla said, her voice barely above a whisper. "Where is he?"

Keisha's expression darkened, and she hesitated before answering. "He ain't here, Priscilla. He been gone."

Priscilla's heart sank, but she hadn't expected as much. Marcus had been made it clear he was done, but she hadn't realized just how far he had gone until now. "He left me for good, didn't he?"

Keisha nodded, her eyes filled with sympathy. "He did more than that, girl. I ain't wanna tell you this while you was laid up in here, but you need to know the truth."

Priscilla braced herself, knowing that whatever Keisha was about to say would hurt, but needing to hear it anyway. "Tell me."

Keisha sighed, her voice heavy with the weight of what she was about to reveal. "Marcus been seein' another woman. He wit some young thing, part of that circle y'all used to run in. Word is, he planned on moving outta the state with her and said he didn't give a fuck about you before he bounced."

The words hit Priscilla like a punch to the gut. But it was 100 times worse hearing it while she lay bleeding in a hospital bed—it was almost too much to bear.

Priscilla's throat tightened, and she fought back the tears threatening to spill over. "Why didn't he just come check on me? Why'd he have to do me like that?"

Keisha reached out, placing a comforting hand on Priscilla's arm. "Some people ain't got no heart, Priscilla. Marcus was lookin' out for himself he don't care about nothing or nobody."

Priscilla swallowed hard, her mind racing with the betrayal, the lies, the pain. She had lost everything—her sister, her marriage, her life as she knew it.

"Fuck him them," Priscilla said, her voice trembling. "I can't be that nice person anymore."

Keisha nodded, understanding in her eyes. "Then don't. You gotta start over, Priscilla. Build somethin' new, somethin' better. Leave him and all this shit behind."

Priscilla took a deep breath, letting the truth of Keisha's words sink in. She had been holding on to a life that was already gone, trying to piece together something that was never going to be whole again. But now, she knew she had to let it go. She had to find a way to move forward, to create a new life out of the ashes of the old one.

As the days passed, Priscilla began to heal, not just physically, but emotionally as well. She filed for divorce, cutting the last ties to Marcus and the life they had once shared. It was painful, but it was necessary. She couldn't keep holding on to something that was already dead.

Rachel's trial came and went, and the sentence was harsh—20 years, with no chance of parole. The judge felt with her criminal record she was a threat to society. Priscilla visited her once, hoping to find some closure, some way to say goodbye to the sister she had lost. But Rachel was distant, her eyes cold and unfeeling, the person she hoped she would be was gone.

"I'm sorry," Priscilla had whispered through the thick glass separating them, her heart breaking all over again.

Rachel had only stared at her, her expression unreadable. "It's too late for sorry, Priscilla. You can't change what happened. Ain't no fixin' this."

Priscilla had left the prison with a heavy heart, knowing that she had done all she could, but it hadn't been enough. The streets had claimed Rachel, and there was nothing more she could do.

Back in the city, Priscilla began to rebuild her life, slowly but surely. She was given a settlement in the divorce, and she found a small apartment, nothing like the mansion she had once lived in, but it was hers. She started working again, taking on small jobs, trying to find her footing in a world that had once seemed so foreign to her.

Keisha stayed by her side, helping her through the dark days, reminding her that she wasn't alone. And as the months passed, Priscilla began to feel something she hadn't felt in a long time—hope.

But the scars of the past remained, a constant reminder of the battle she had fought and the losses she had suffered. The streets had left their mark on her, and she knew she would never be the same. But she also knew that she had survived, and that was something.

As she stood on the balcony of her new apartment, looking out over the city, Priscilla felt a sense of peace wash over her. The pain was still there, the sadness, the betrayal, but so was the strength. She had faced the darkness and come out on the other side, battered but not broken.

Chapter 18: Secrets and Lies

Priscilla had thought she'd finally found some peace, a sense of closure after everything that had happened. She had begun to rebuild her life from the ashes, piece by piece, hoping that the worst was behind her.

She received a phone call. The number was unknown, the voice on the other end unfamiliar but full of urgency. "You Priscilla, right? I got somethin' you need to know. Meet me at the old warehouse on Ninth. You know the one. Be there at midnight."

Before she could respond, the line went dead, leaving Priscilla staring at her phone, a cold feeling creeping up her spine. She didn't recognize the voice, but there was something about it—something that told her this was serious, that she couldn't ignore it.

She had just started getting her life back on track, but the some how it seemed shit just wouldn't end. What was this about?

Keisha tried to talk her out of it, her voice filled with concern. "Girl, you don't need to go chasin' no more trouble. You done enough of that. Let the past stay buried."

But Priscilla couldn't shake the feeling that this was important, that she needed to know whatever this person had to tell her. "I gotta go, Keisha. Somethin' tells me I need to hear what they have to say."

That night, Priscilla found herself back in the part of the city she had been trying to forget—the part where secrets thrived in the shadows, where lies festered like wounds that never healed. The part of town was as grim as she remembered, its walls covered in graffiti, the windows shattered, allowing the cold night air to seep through.

She stepped inside the warehouse, the floor creaking under her feet, the darkness closing in around her like an old, familiar enemy. The place was empty, but the tension in the air was thick, almost suffocating. She was alone, but she knew someone was watching her, waiting for the right moment to reveal themselves.

"You came," the voice from the phone call echoed through the empty space, making Priscilla tense. A figure stepped out of the shadows, a woman with a hard, weathered face, eyes that had seen too much.

Priscilla narrowed her eyes, trying to place the woman. "Who are you? And what do you want with me?"

The woman stepped closer, her gaze never leaving Priscilla's. "Name's Gloria. I heard what happened with you and you sister and I knew your mama. The real one."

Priscilla's heart skipped a beat at the mention of her mother. "What do you mean? You knew her?"

Gloria nodded, her expression grim. "I was there, back in the day. Saw how things went down. I know the truth 'bout your family, 'bout how you and Rachel really ended up where you did."

Priscilla's blood ran cold. She had already uncovered so much about her past, but the idea that there was more, that there were still secrets hidden in the darkness—it shook her to her core. "What truth? What are you talkin' about?"

Gloria sighed, as if the weight of the truth was almost too much to bear. "Your mama was deep in some bad shit. She was a junkie, but it was worse than that. She was mixed up with some bad people—people who wanted more than just a few favors. She owed them, and when she couldn't pay, they took what they wanted."

Priscilla felt her stomach churn. "What did they take?"

Gloria looked her dead in the eyes. "You."

The word hung in the air like a death sentence, and Priscilla felt the ground shift beneath her feet. "What the hell do you mean?"

"Your mama didn't sell you off 'cause she wanted to. She didn't have a choice. Those people she was mixed up with? They wanted a baby, wanted to raise one up their own way, use 'em for God knows what. She gave you to them to save her own skin. Rachel wasn't part of the deal. They didn't want her, so she got left behind."

Priscilla's mind reeled, the pieces of her past shifting into a new, horrifying picture. "So I was... what, taken?"

Gloria nodded, her face dark with the memories. "Yeah, you was. But your mama tried to get you back. She went to war with them folks, did everything she could. But they was too powerful, too deep in the game. By the time she found a way out, you was gone, livin' with your new folks, and she couldn't get close."

Priscilla's heart raced as the truth sank in. Her entire life had been built on lies, on a twisted story that had been fed to her from the day she was born. And the woman she had grown up calling "mother" had been part of that lie, part of the cover-up.

"But why didn't she come for me? Why didn't she try to get me back?" Priscilla demanded, her voice shaking with anger and confusion.

Gloria shook her head. "She tried, but they threatened her, threatened to kill Rachel if she didn't back off. Your mama loved you both, but she was stuck, trapped by the life she had chosen. She couldn't get you back without losin' Rachel, so she did the only thing she could. She let you go."

Priscilla's vision blurred with tears as the reality of her mother's choices hit her like a sledgehammer. Her mother had sacrificed everything to keep her and Rachel safe, but in the end, the streets had still claimed them both.

"And what about Rachel?" Priscilla asked, her voice barely a whisper.

"Rachel didn't know the whole story," Gloria said, her voice heavy with regret. "She knew she was left behind, knew you got away, but she never knew the why. She grew up hatin' you for what she thought you had, never knowin' the truth of what really went down."

Priscilla felt her world crumbling around her. Everything she had believed, everything she had built her life on, was a lie. The truth had been buried for so long, hidden behind layers of secrets and deception, and now it was all coming to light.

Gloria stepped closer, her voice low and urgent. "I'm tellin' you this 'cause you need to know the truth. You need to understand where you come from, what's in your blood. The streets, they got a hold on your sister, just like they had a hold on your mama. I can give you the address to the old office building you can find information you need there."

Chapter 19: A Twisted Conclusion

The city was quiet, almost too quiet, as Priscilla walked down the cracked sidewalk, the weight of everything that had happened pressing down on her shoulders. The rain had finally stopped for a moment, leaving the streets glistening under the dim streetlights. The silence was heavy, like the calm before a storm.

She had been trying to find some semblance of normalcy after everything that had gone down, but normalcy felt like a distant memory, something that belonged to someone else, not her. The streets had taken too much from her, and the scars ran deep. But there was still one last piece of the puzzle she had to face, one last secret that had been gnawing at her ever since Gloria's revelation.

Priscilla had spent the last few days digging, searching through old records, trying to make sense of the twisted history that had bound her and Rachel together in a web of hatred, lies and betrayal. And now, she was on her way to put another piece of truth to the puzzle.

She arrived at an address Gloria had given her and old office building on the edge of the neighborhood, its stone walls worn and weathered by time. The place was abandoned, the windows boarded up, but it had a presence, an aura of secrets long buried. It was here that everything had started, and it was here that everything would end.

Priscilla pushed open the heavy wooden door, the creak echoing through the empty space. The air inside was cold, damp, and smelled of decay, but she didn't flinch. She walked down the center aisle, her footsteps echoing off the stone walls, until she reached an old desk. There, she found what she had been looking for—an old, tattered book, its pages yellowed with age, resting in a dusty drawer.

Her heart pounded in her chest as she opened the book, her fingers trembling. The pages were filled with handwritten notes, records of transactions, names, dates. It was all there—the proof of what Gloria had told her, the final piece of the puzzle that would reveal the truth once and for all.

As she flipped through the pages, her eyes caught a name—her mother's name. And next to it, a date. The date she had been taken. But there was something else, something that made her blood run cold. Another name, scribbled in the margins, almost as an afterthought.

Rachel.

Priscilla's hands shook as she traced the letters, the realization hitting her like a freight train. The truth was darker than she had ever imagined, more twisted than she could have ever prepared for. Rachel hadn't just been left behind—she had been sold off to cover up a secret even more horrific.

Her mother hadn't given her up to save herself. She had given Priscilla away because she couldn't bear the shame of what she had done. Rachel wasn't her sister by blood. They weren't twins at all. Rachel was the child of an affair, the product of a moment of weakness, and her mother had tried to erase that mistake by arranging a shady adoption to cover her tracks.

Priscilla stumbled back, the book slipping from her fingers and crashing to the floor. Her mind raced as she tried to process the truth, but it was too much. Her whole life had been a lie, her identity a fabrication built on secrets and shame. And now, she was left with the devastating reality that everything she thought, everything she had believed in, had been built on a foundation of lies.

As she stood there, numb and broken, she heard the sound of footsteps behind her. She turned to see Keisha standing in the doorway. She had come to make sure things were good.

"Keisha," Priscilla whispered, her voice barely audible.

Priscilla sobbing, tears streaming down her face. "We're not... we're not sisters. Not really."

Keisha's eyes widened in shock. "What you talkin' 'bout?"

Priscilla shook her head, her voice trembling. " It's all a lie. My momma, she... she gave us away to cover up what she did. Rachel ain't my blood, Keisha. She never was."

Priscilla stood there, the truth still heavy in her chest, her mind reeling from the shock of of all the things that had happened. The secrets and lies that had defined their lives had finally come to light, but the cost was enormous.

The rain began to fall again, the sound of it tapping against the windows like a soft, mournful dirge. Priscilla closed her eyes, letting the tears flow freely, her heart heavy with grief and guilt.

As the rain poured down outside, Priscilla knew that she would never be the same. The truth had changed her, broken her in ways she couldn't yet comprehend.

Priscilla took a deep breath, trying to steady herself. "I don't know what to do, Keisha. I don't even know who I am anymore."

Keisha reached out, taking Priscilla's hand in hers. "You still you, Priscilla. No matter what happened, you still the same person you always been. And you still got people who care 'bout you.

Priscilla closed her eyes, letting the tears flow freely, her heart heavy with grief and guilt. But she also felt something else—a flicker of resolve.

As Keisha stood beside her, her presence a comforting anchor in the storm of emotions swirling inside her, Priscilla knew in that moment that she would never ever be the same.

Keisha squeezed Priscilla's hand tighter, her eyes filled with a mix of sympathy and urgency. "Priscilla, there's somethin' I gotta tell you. I came lookin' for you 'cause... it's about Rachel."

Priscilla's heart skipped a beat, fear clawing at her insides. "What about Rachel?" she asked, her voice barely a whisper.

Keisha hesitated, her face etched with grief. "She's gone, Priscilla. Rachel... she got stabbed in prison. She didn't make it."

The words hit Priscilla like a punch to the gut, the air rushing out of her lungs. "No... no, that can't be," she stammered, shaking her head in disbelief. "Rachel... she can't be gone. Not like this."

"I'm sorry, Priscilla," Keisha said softly, tears welling up in her eyes. "I know this ain't easy to hear, but you needed to know. I'm here for you, no matter what."

Priscilla felt her legs give way, collapsing onto the cold, damp floor. The weight of everything—Rachel's death, the lies about their family, the betrayal and loss—crashed down on her all at once, and she sobbed uncontrollably, her body wracked with grief.

Keisha knelt beside her, wrapping her arms around Priscilla and holding her close. "I know it hurts, Priscilla. I know you feel like you're drownin' right now, but you gotta keep goin' shit is just fucked up right now."

Priscilla clung to Keisha, the tears flowing freely down her face.

She took a deep, shuddering breath, trying to steady herself. "I don't know how, Keisha," she whispered, her voice cracking. "I don't know how to keep goin' when everything's so fucked up."

Keisha pulled back slightly, looking Priscilla in the eyes. "You just take it one day at a time, sis. One breath at a time. And you remember that you got people who love you, who need you to keep pushin'. We'll get through this together, I promise."

As she stood up, leaning on Keisha for support, Priscilla wiped the tears from her eyes and took a deep, steadying breath. "Thank you, Keisha. For bein' here."

Keisha nodded, giving Priscilla's hand one last squeeze. "You're my family, Priscilla. Always. And I'm gonna be right here with you, every step of the way."

The two women stood together in the empty, abandoned building, the rain still tapping softly against the windows. Priscilla knew that this chapter of her life had come to a painful, tragic end.

With a heavy heart but a determined spirit, Priscilla turned and walked out of the building with Keisha, stepping into the rain-soaked streets. She didn't know what the future held, but she was ready to face it head-on. It was time to close this chapter and start a new one—a chapter where she would define her own destiny, free from the shadows of the past. Free from theses blues.

Don't miss out!

Visit the website below and you can sign up to receive emails whenever Rachael Reed publishes a new book. There's no charge and no obligation.

https://books2read.com/r/B-A-WXARB-RNCYE

BOOKS 2 READ

Connecting independent readers to independent writers.

Did you love *Trail Ride Blues*? Then you should read *Can't Turn a Hoe Into a Housewife*[1] by Rachael Reed!

[2]

In the gritty streets of the city, where loyalty is tested and danger lurks around every corner, Can't Turn a Hoe into a Housewife dives deep into the underbelly of urban life. Erica, a seasoned escort with a sharp mind and a guarded heart, dreams of escaping the fast life and finding something real. But in a world where money rules and trust is scarce, her journey ain't easy.

When Erica crosses paths with Quan, a man with a genuine heart and a promise of love, she sees a glimmer of hope. But leaving the game ain't simple, especially with a ruthless pimp like Lil Ron, who ain't about to let his top girl go without a fight. As Erica tries to walk the line

---

1. https://books2read.com/u/4XdEN1

2. https://books2read.com/u/4XdEN1

between her old life and a new beginning, Lil Ron tightens his grip, turning their lives into a deadly game of cat and mouse.

Can't Turn a Hoe into a Housewife is a tale of love, betrayal, and survival in a world where the streets don't play fair. With a dark, raw tone and a cast of characters struggling against their circumstances, this story is packed with twists, drama, and the harsh reality of street life. As Erica fights to break free and find redemption, the stakes get higher, and the danger becomes all too real.

In this urban fiction thriller, the line between right and wrong blurs, and every choice comes with a price. Will Erica escape the life that's bound her, or will the streets claim her for good? Get ready for a cliffhanging ride through the hood, where love ain't always enough to save you from your past.

Also by Rachael Reed

Sis
Sis 2 Blood on the Streets

Standalone
Codefendant
Codefendant
Once a Cheater
Once a Cheater
Passport Bro
What Happens in Prison
Preference
Sprinkle Sprinkle
Championship Bad
Street Exodus
Street Exodus
Street Royalty
Pawns of Power
SIS
Cartel Bloodline
Get Money Girls
Skip the Games
Til Death Do Us Part

Backpage Hustle
Link in Bio
The Virgin and The Kingpin
A Gangsta's Heart
Boosters
Can't Turn a Hoe Into a Housewife
Better you Than Me
Wig Dealer: How to Start Your wig Business
Trail Ride Blues

www.ingramcontent.com/pod-product-compliance
Lightning Source LLC
Chambersburg PA
CBHW051446140726
47987CB00006B/2561